"How long would we have to pretend to be married?"

"Not long. Within a few weeks, we'll issue a statement that the media attention is putting too much pressure on our marriage and we're taking a break. Do you need a lawyer?" He picked up his phone.

For a marriage that wasn't real? Bianca's brain was tripping over her heart, trying not to hit the hard ground of how quickly he was planning on dumping her:

"And what—" She cleared her throat. "What are the rules?"

"Rules?"

"You told me to move into your room. What do you expect will happen there?" She sat straighter, affecting a look of objective interest, but her pulse was swerving all over the map.

She didn't know what answer she was hoping for. Yes, she did. No, she didn't. Did she want to sleep with him again? Yes. But no. She wanted to sleep with the man he'd been the first time they met, the one who wasn't so enigmatic and remote. She wanted to be the woman she used to be, the one with a life and a career, friends and a home. One who knew who she was. These days, she was a stray. An orphan. A pariah in some circles. A ghost of the woman she'd been.

Canadian **Dani Collins** knew in high school that she wanted to write romance for a living. Twenty-five years later, after marrying her high school sweetheart, having two kids with him, working at several generic office jobs and submitting countless manuscripts, she got The Call. Her first Harlequin novel won the Reviewers' Choice Award for Best First in Series from *RT Book Reviews*. She now works in her own office, writing romance.

Books by Dani Collins

Harlequin Presents

Confessions of an Italian Marriage
Innocent in the Sheikh's Palace
What the Greek's Wife Needs
Her Impossible Baby Bombshell
One Snowbound New Year's Night

Signed, Sealed...Seduced

Ways to Ruin a Royal Reputation

The Secret Sisters

Married for One Reason Only
Manhattan's Most Scandalous Reunion

Visit the Author Profile page
at Harlequin.com for more titles.

Dani Collins

CINDERELLA FOR
THE MIAMI PLAYBOY

ISBN-13: 978-1-335-56950-9

Cinderella for the Miami Playboy

Copyright © 2022 by Dani Collins

Harlequin Enterprises ULC
22 Adelaide St. West, 41st Floor
Toronto, Ontario M5H 4E3, Canada
www.Harlequin.com

Printed in U.S.A.

CINDERELLA FOR
THE MIAMI PLAYBOY

To all the readers who asked me if Everett from *Confessions of an Italian Marriage* would get his own story, this one's for you! xo

PROLOGUE

New York, six months ago...

EVERETT DRAKE WAS in the worst possible mood for a man like him. He was *bored*. Bored was one step away from making trouble purely to stay awake.

You're lucky. *You'll enjoy it*, had been the refrain from the few people who knew of his retirement. *I'm so glad you're out of it*, his mother had said of the end of his career handling agents and informants for the U.S. Government.

He was not glad. He was livid. Men twice his age moved to Miami to tinker with cars. He was in the prime of his life and ought to be doing something more meaningful, but he couldn't. Wouldn't. He was punishing himself and that was as it should be. He would live quietly. *Authentically*. The way normal people lived.

Well, normal people with buckets of wealth from multiple sources. Given his deep pockets, he could do anything he wanted, even be the dissolute playboy he had used as his cover for the last fifteen years.

Nothing about any of that appealed, though. Not the travel, not the parties. It was all empty as hell. He couldn't even race cars or hydrofoils. His mother would drag him out by the collar and run him over herself.

Given his current ennui, that didn't sound half-bad.

He gave up his overnight bag to the flight attendant as he climbed aboard the executive jet. The automotive parts he'd come to New York to source himself—because he was that desperate for something to do—were already stowed below.

Old habits had him glancing at the manifest to read the names of his fellow passengers. Only one. Bianca Palmer. The name was unfamiliar, and it didn't matter, he reminded himself. He was no longer on guard against those who might seek to unmask him, or digging to find those who carried secrets like smuggled cargo.

He stepped into the main cabin, glanced at the woman in the luxury armchair on the left and a thousand impressions hit him at once, many of them the visceral reaction of a healthy male spotting an apparently fertile female. Alluring curves on a lithe build. Slender calves beneath a narrow skirt. Her ankles were crossed carefully to avoid scuffing her designer shoes. Her silk blouse was open at her throat, providing a view of her honey-gold upper chest, unadorned by any chain or locket.

That other more analytic part of him noted that her clothes were priced comparably to the bespoke suit and Italian shoes he wore. He judged her age at seven or eight years younger than his thirty-five. She was a professional, but not in a conservative career like banking. Something creative, given the way her rich brunette hair was side-parted and woven into a braid from one ear around the back of her head to the other, ending in a wavy waterfall behind her hoop earring.

She understood the value of appearances and how a style like that conveyed an eye for beauty and attention to detail. Sophisticated makeup emphasized her features. Bronze dusted her eyelids and playful cat tails decorated the corners of her eyes. Her complexion was a flawless, golden tan, almost olive. Her nose held an elegant curve at the bridge and her jawline was strong yet very feminine. Merlot-colored lipstick coated her wide mouth, glossy enough that her lips looked kiss-dampened and pillowy. Inviting.

Her dark chocolate gaze lifted absently from dropping something into her handbag and locked with his for no reason other than that they were sexually compatible. He wasn't coy about such things. He had been told many times he was handsome, and he had zero problems dressing well and shaving daily to heighten that impression. She was vibrant and beautiful, and chemistry was a wonderful thing when it struck both parties equally, as it was doing right now.

A satisfying billow of desire moved through his chest like smoke before sinking into his belly and groin.

He watched her throat flex as she swallowed. Her eyes widened slightly before her gaze flickered all over him like an indecisive butterfly, leaving tickling touches at his shoulders and the middle of his chest, on to his tense abdomen and lower, following the sharp crease in his trousers to his freshly shined shoes.

As her gaze made its way back, the delicious tightness of arousal invaded the flesh behind his fly and climbed his spine, releasing an urge to pursue into his blood.

"Good morning," he greeted.

"Good morning." Her voice held a husky note. He wasn't sure if it was natural or because they were having such an effect on each other. She dropped her gaze into her lap, where she was twisting her fingers.

A fresh impression struck him like a slap, one that was an even sharper cat nip than carnal hunger. He read tension, vulnerability, wariness. *Secrets.*

The hair on the back of his neck lifted, and

there was a tang in his nostrils like the whiff off an extinguished match.

His ability to scent danger had kept him and others alive more often than he could count—and that one time when he had ignored it—

No.

He brushed that incident aside, staying in the moment because that's how you stayed alive when this happened, but his sexual interest had collided straight into that part of him he had severed like a limb. The part that chased intrigue and answers and knew that knowledge was power. The part that *liked* that power and enjoyed skating on the edge of icy cliffs.

He was an addict. That's what he was. Whatever was going on with this woman was nothing to do with him. *Ignore her. Go live your life*, he ordered himself.

What life, though? The banality of his existence was likely to kill him quicker than his old life might have, but he had made his choices. He would live with the consequences.

"May I bring champagne? Mimosas?" The flight attendant arrived behind him and accepted the jacket he removed.

"Nothing for me, thank you," Bianca said in her sensual voice.

"Coffee," Everett requested, and seated himself across from her, resisting the urge to swivel his chair so he could see her better. Not for him. Not today. Not ever.

Bianca turned her face to the window and knotted her hands in her lap.

Ringless hands, Everett noted. Why couldn't there be a band or a diamond there? He would have dismissed his attraction without another thought. Even in his previous life, he only lied as much as he absolutely had to. Entangling himself with a woman who happened to be cheating on her partner fell into unnecessary deceit.

But given the absence of rings or last-minute texting or chatty *I love yous* before switching to airplane mode, his libido urged him to make a pass. He didn't get nearly as much sex as the profligate playboy he pretended to be. If she was amenable, why the hell shouldn't he spend a night with her? He could stay at a hotel rather than take her home. Keep it to one night.

Just one drink. Just dinner. Just enough to find out what her story was.

It truly was the rationalization of someone with a substance abuse problem. Just *no.*

He was so damned aware of her, though. It was as if he sat next to a radiator that softly pinged as it baked his right side.

The ladder came up and the seal of the door locked them into a bubble of charged air. He knew she was chewing her bottom lip. Her head was still tilted toward the window, but he knew she was as aware of him as he was of her. A special sort of tension emanated off her. He knew she was sliding surreptitious glances from the corner of her eye because he was doing the same.

Nope, nope, nope.

Was he even reading her correctly? Or was his latent horniness tasting all this electricity and turning it into something it wasn't? Maybe she was just a nervous flyer.

As the plane taxied and the attendant buckled into her own seat for takeoff, he remarked, "I use this charter company all the time. These jets are very reliable. You won't feel any turbulence."

In fact, he owned shares in the company. In his previous life, he would volunteer a detail like that. He had always liked to nurture the impression his fortune was inherited, passive and mildly obnoxious. That way he avoided inconvenient questions about what he did for a living. People presumed "nothing."

That's exactly what he did now, but he balked at this woman viewing him as shallow and aimless. He wasn't sure why. It rarely bothered him what anyone thought of him.

She shot him a culpable glance, seeming briefly rattled before she visibly took hold of herself, stacking her hands and relaxing her shoulders, pasting on a smile.

"Am I that obvious?"

Wow. That blanket of false calm was such a deliberate application of control, as though she were sitting in a high-stakes poker game and realized she was betraying herself with a tell. His most sharply honed synapses fired in his brain.

Definitely not this one, his logic brain said firmly.

His lizard brain shifted his ankle onto his knee, hiding the fact he was growing hard. She was caressing all his buttons with that serene mask that disguised a mystery and the way her breath subtly hitched, causing her breasts to quiver.

"Allow me to distract you," he suggested. Because if he was going to fall off the wagon, it ought to be with premium, hundred-year-old Scotch, right? *Look at her.* "Are you heading to Miami for business or pleasure? Visiting family?"

Surprise bloomed behind her eyes as she realized he was hitting on her.

He didn't like to waste time, he informed her with a sideways pull of his mouth, but how could she be surprised? Women with that much sex appeal were inundated with advances. They knew how to shut them down very quickly and he always respected that, but he found himself holding his breath as he awaited her reaction.

She blinked in disconcertion, and her finger and thumb worked the spot at the base of her naked ring finger as she considered how to handle his attention.

Ah. There was no ring, but there was a commitment in place, one that typically shielded her from sexual interest. Pity.

It was for the best—he knew it was—but he couldn't remember ever feeling his inner animal rising so urgently with desire. He made himself sip his hot coffee to burn away the pall of disappointment in the back of his throat.

She didn't mention a partner, however. Nor did she grasp at the armrest or show any sort of nerves as the engine roar grew and the plane gathered speed. She seemed perfectly relaxed as they were pressed into their seats by the climbing jet.

He didn't take credit for taking her mind off her trepidation, though. Flying wasn't what she was afraid of. He knew that in his gut, but all his willpower seemed to have been left on the ground. His entire being was awake and alive in a way he hadn't been in months.

"I'm not sure how to answer," she confided as they leveled off, forcing his mind back to the question he'd asked. "It's a little bit of all of those. Business, pleasure and family. My grandmother passed recently."

"I'm sorry," he said politely.

"I didn't know her," she dismissed, but the corners of her mouth briefly tilted down. "She stopped speaking to my mother when Mom got pregnant and wasn't married. We reached out a few times, but we never heard back. Then, out of the blue, I got a letter saying my grandmother had left me her apartment. I'm going to Miami to sell it."

Her glance reflected resignation and... Damn. He knew that cagey look. She was hoping he was satisfied with what she'd given him. She was holding something back.

They were strangers, though. Sometimes that allowed a person to open up without reserve, but not all the time. Family was complicated, and convoluted stories didn't always reap useful information. He left room for her to elaborate by saying, "That sounds troubling."

"It is. Thank you for acknowledging that." Her brows came together with annoyance. "Everyone seems to think I've won the lottery. All I can think is that I would have preferred a relationship with her. I mean, she didn't even send me a card when her *daughter* died, but she made me her beneficiary? That's bizarre, isn't it?"

Perhaps that was the source of her tension. Her conscience must be bothered by accepting a windfall from someone who had hurt her mother.

"You can never be sure why someone holds others at arm's length. Shame. Anger. Secrets."

Self-loathing. Guilt. Everett eschewed intimate relationships for all of those reasons.

"I know, but…" Her mouth twisted with frustration.

This time, as their gazes met, a deeper curiosity crept into her expression, one that stoked the heat in his gut. Her attention strayed over his clean-shaven face again and reassessed his shoulders and chest and thighs, all of which he ruthlessly kept in fighting form.

She tellingly eyed his left hand, which bore neither ring nor tan line.

Everett had tried long-term relationships. They had always withered from neglect, mostly due to work getting in the way. He had all the time in the world now, though, and a soft blush of attraction had risen under her skin, one that pleased him immensely as did the implied interest in her next words.

"And you? Why are you going to Miami?"

I live there. That's what he should have said, but old instincts had him prevaricating.

"There's a yacht I'm thinking of buying. I'm only in town the one night—" He always liked to be clear about his limitations and in this case, he should have shut his mouth ten minutes ago, but there was a war going on inside him. He knew, *he knew* not to ignore the way his scalp was tightening, but his interest in her was galloping like a wild stallion, determined to catch her and have her.

Lust won over logic.

"I'll be free by six and dining alone unless you'd like to join me?"

Her head tilted as she considered his invitation. For one second, he had the impression of looking in a mirror. She was definitely hiding more than she was revealing.

Tension invaded his muscles. He ought to be hoping for a rebuff. It rarely happened, but when it did, it didn't bother him. If she turned him down, however, he would be more than disappointed. He'd be thwarted.

Her guardedness relaxed a few notches as she offered a shy smile. "I would like that." She leaned out to offer her hand. "I'm Bianca, by the way."

As he took her hand, a punch of desire struck his middle. Her breath caught as though she experienced a similar impact. He swept his thumb across the back of her knuckles before releasing her, absorbing the fact she posed a type of danger he hadn't ever experienced.

He really should retract and retreat. This was madness.

"Everett," he provided. "I'll make a reservation at my hotel."

CHAPTER ONE

Present day, Miami

BIANCA PALMER HAD what anyone would consider an ideal job, especially when one was hiding from the law, reporters and the white-collar criminals she had implicated when she had blown the whistle on them.

She hadn't known what to expect when she had pulled a number off the We Can Find You Work flyer at the bodega near the sketchy room she'd been renting by the week, but Miami had a thriving underground economy. There were tons of companies that placed undocumented workers in domestic positions. Her desire for cash-only employment hadn't raised any eyebrows and when she had offered a generous bonus for "extra privacy," the manager had taken her pay-off as a sweetener and sent her to interview for this cushy gig.

Despite the blue pixie cut she'd given herself when she had abandoned her old life, she'd been terrified she would be recognized, so she had also worn gray contacts and appropriated an old school friend's Puerto Rican accent. After spinning a story about supporting her ailing grandmother, she had landed the position.

She lived in the pool house of a mansion on Miami's Indian Creek. It wasn't the most extravagant house in the neighborhood, but it was very swanky with two cabanas next to its free-form pool, five bedrooms in the main house, nine baths, a home theater and an elevator to a rooftop bar. The six-car garage held a motorcycle, an SUV, a modern sports car in pristine condition and two vintage ones in different states of restoration. The last bay was taken up with shelves of tools and parts.

Those fancy cars, virtually the only personal items she'd seen here, were extremely well protected. Every door and window of the house was wired and alarmed. A high brick wall surrounded the property and surveillance cameras monitored every exterior angle, including the path to the private beach where no watercraft were moored.

That always made her wonder. The dock was built for a large yacht, but there wasn't even a little runabout. Of course, no one came or went from the road, either. The woman who had hired her—a housekeeper who had possibly hired Bianca for cash so she could take time off while her employers were away—had said the house was being held in trust while the owners were in divorce proceedings.

Bianca hadn't asked for more information than that. It was too sweet a deal. Her accommodation was part of her compensation and her duties consisted of dusting, vacuuming, mowing the small patch of lawn and polishing the windows.

There were *so many* windows, probably with a square footage equal to the house. They all looked onto stunning views and were all tinted against the intense Florida sunshine. Bianca was well shielded from view if she wanted to stand in the main lounge next to the grand piano and speculate on what all those people in those skyscrapers in Miami Beach were doing as they went about their very normal lives.

She tried not to do that. It made her yearn to drag heavy bags onto the crowded subway and overhear lively conversations in languages she didn't recognize. She wanted to drink in spicy food aromas mixed with the gritty stench of city streets and walk through a door calling out, *"I'm home!"*

She wanted someone to answer her back.

Instead, she skimmed the pool or did her yoga practice beneath the weighted branches of the orange trees and tried to convince herself this isolation was a gift. She was paid well *and* had a generous budget for groceries and household incidentals. Deliveries were left at the gate, allowing her to live expense-free and undetected.

It was a bizarre arrangement that she had leaped on when she'd been desperate for a means to support herself while staying out of sight. Now that she'd had time to dwell on it—seriously, nothing but time to dwell—she wondered if she had leaped out of the frying pan of financial fraud only to land in a roaring fire of something equally unsavory. That would make her not only an accessory, which she was trying to avoid, but also the world's biggest hypocrite. Who exposed crimes only to assist in different ones?

Was the owner of this house a criminal? Wealthy people could be felons. Bianca knew that from her experience with Morris and Ackerley. Her fiancé had been a charming, Ivy League alum with generations of wealth behind him, but he'd still cheated average citizens out of their life savings.

She felt like such a fool for getting involved with him! For believing his flattery and letting him take advantage of her grief.

Thanks to her poor judgment, she didn't have much choice even if she *was* being paid with dirty money. She'd made her bed and would have to keep sleeping in it.

With a sigh, she picked the ripe oranges and

took them to the main kitchen, as she did every morning. She made her toast and ate it while she squeezed juice that she would freeze in ice cube trays. They made a nice addition to a glass of water or white wine, but she didn't have enough room in her small fridge to keep it all there.

As she worked, she daydreamed about where she would go if she could leave. It was one of her preoccupations every single day, along with what sort of career she should retrain for since she had nuked her old one. Where and how could she start over, and would anyone want anything to do with her?

It was hard being inside her head all the time. She was hideously lonely. Aside from answering the intercom when drivers notified her of deliveries, she hadn't spoken to anyone since the day she'd taken this job. She barely interacted with the outside world at all, staying offline and buying paperback romance novels and DVDs with her groceries.

At first, she had watched the news incessantly, but she could barely make herself do even that these days. Morris and Ackerley were being investigated, which was what she had wanted, but progress was glacial. The company was denying and deflecting and throwing mud on her name at every opportunity.

It was exactly what she had expected them to do, but it was hard to watch her character being assassinated. It made her want to defend herself, but no matter how tempted she was, she never, ever, *ever* reached out to anyone or checked her social media feeds.

Or checked up on *him*.

Everett.

Her eyes drifted shut in a mixture of reminiscence and mortification. After meeting him on the plane to Miami, she had looked him up at the library while making her final preparations toward abandoning her old life. She'd still been of two minds as to whether she should meet him for dinner.

According to the tabloid articles, his father had been a renowned automotive engineer from Switzerland, who suffered a brain injury during a test drive. His French mother had been an interpreter at the UN. There had been scads of family money that had mostly come to Everett in his early twenties.

With all that gold falling out of his pockets, he had become a playboy in the most iconic sense. He traveled the globe on spontaneous adventures, seeing and being seen. There had been links to nightclub appearances and ski holidays and affairs with this or that socialite. For a time, he had raced cars. There had been a youthful photo of him in Monte Carlo, shirtless and with his arms around two extremely beautiful women dressed in gold shorts and eyelet bikini tops.

I wonder what he would think of those cars in the garage, Bianca sometimes mused.

She thought of him far too often, almost as if he was her companion here. It was an odd trick that her mind played on her, probably because she was so starved for company and because he was the last person with whom she'd had a meaningful interaction.

Meaningful, Bianca? For her, perhaps, but it had been obvious from the first moment that he was a serial pickup artist. Joining him for dinner had served her own purpose, but she had meant for it to only be dinner. Hookups with strangers weren't her style *at all*.

He'd had a charming way about him, though, one that disarmed and encouraged her to trust him. He had fascinated her with his intelligence and nuanced opinions while drawing her out with what seemed like genuine interest in her. It had taken superhuman effort not to blurt out what she was about to do. Only her lifetime of keeping secrets had allowed her to compartmentalize and leave him in the dark.

Even so, she'd been in a heightened state, fearful of what she was about to do and eager for the distraction he offered. Given the huge step she had been about to undertake, it made sense that she had taken another uncharacteristic risk of letting a stranger seduce her.

Maybe she'd simply needed to be held.

Either way, that interlude should have made her feel empty and used, but she had reveled in it, letting go of herself completely. It had been a unique experience where the outer layers of her persona had seemed to burn away in the heat of their passion. When she had left his room, she had walked away altered at her deepest level. Centered and confident. New.

Or she was completely delusional, and he'd just been really good in bed.

She longed to see him again and find out. A far more sensible part of her suspected she would be hideously disappointed if she met him again. She doubted he had spared a single thought for her. He might not even remember her, which would be humiliating in the extreme.

Leaving here wasn't an option anyway. She would be mobbed by paparazzi, if the way reporters were badgering Troy was any indication. All the letters of the alphabet seemed to be looking for her—SEC, FBI, DOJ. From what she'd seen of other whistleblowers' experiences, she could face prosecution or be persecuted for leaking information. If she was offered protection, she would likely wind up exactly as she was, cut off from the world but with less agency. Most importantly, if Troy Ackerley and his partner, Kirk Morris, got their hands on her, the outcome could be life-threatening.

No, she was safest exactly where she was,

even if she was claustrophobic and lonesome and bordering on despair.

She twisted the orange half with excessive force, trying not to cry.

Oh, stop it. She jammed the last of her toast into her mouth, not caring that her juice-coated fingers gave the PBJ a weird, tangy flavor. Pity parties solved nothing. She swallowed away the lump of toast and reached for the last orange.

As she touched the knife blade to the skin, a soft, measured sound came to her ears, a muted, rhythmic pattern of thumps.

That wasn't the neighbor's sound system. What was it? She held very still, listening, trying to place it. Not a bird or—heaven help her—a gator? One couldn't get in here, could it?

With a lurch of her heart, she realized it was growing louder, coming toward the open sliding door to her left, the one that led onto the courtyard and the paved, poolside dining area.

She never left doors open, only this one, and only when she crossed into this kitchen from her cabana. She always felt safe leaving the screen in place because the courtyard was completely enclosed—except for the single locked gate that accessed the path down to the beach.

That gate was on the same circuit as everything else. She glanced at the computer in the nook beside the pantry. The monitor showed the screen saver, not the view from the cameras the way it was supposed to if motion had triggered the system to start recording.

Something was definitely out there, though. Some*one*?

As the sound closed in, Bianca's breath backed up in her lungs. The wait became macabre. It was timed like footsteps, but that's not what it was. It was longer and slower with a tap and a rest, a tap and—

A man on crutches appeared behind the screen and froze as he spotted her. They stared at one another.

He wore a gray-green shirt with a subtle palm leaf pattern and pale gray shorts, both tailored. His knee was bandaged and so were his knuckles. His cheekbone wore a garish purple shiner, and his eyes narrowed, projecting the warmth of an Ice Age glacier.

Despite all that, buoyant delight slammed through her.

"Everett!" She was ecstatic to see a familiar face, even as concern lurched through her at how banged up he was. She was glad to see *him*, flattered even, after thinking about him so much since—

Reality arrived in a breath-punching tackle. He shouldn't be here. He was from her old life. This was her new one. How had he found her?

Her heart kicked into an unsteady gallop. Her scrambled brain tried to tell her body what to do. Adrenaline seared through her veins like a bullet train, but her muscles turned to stretchy rubber. Think, Bianca. *Run.*

She had a go-bag packed in the cabana, but Everett was swishing the screen open, hitching himself into the kitchen, placing himself between the screen door to the courtyard and the door to the lounge. He sucked all the oxygen from the room with his presence. His gaze flickered around as though searching out hidden dangers.

"Hello, Bianca." His voice was harder than she remembered. His gaze came back to hers, and the easygoing confidence of a lothario had become a force field of power.

Some basic, primitive female in her absorbed that he had become even more appealing. His shoulders seemed broader, and his biceps bulged where he braced on his crutches. The other part noted his scowl was pure Hollywood hit man, sexy enough to turn her bones to pudding, but sending her into survival mode.

She spun and ran through the door into the garage. No bag, no cash, but she had a contingency plan in place for such an emergency. It was a terrible plan, but it was a chance. Her only chance.

She snatched the fob off the hook and ran for the fancy sports car—

"Bianca!" His thunderous shout was accompanied by a clatter.

She reflexively looked over her shoulder, stumbling into the coupe and crashing her hip into its side-view mirror.

"Do not steal my car," he warned in a deadly voice. "That would annoy me, and I am already very annoyed." He was using his shoulder to hold open the door to the kitchen, slouching as he tried to pick up the crutch that had fallen.

"*Your* car." Her brain was trying very hard to think through the miasma of shock and disbelief, fear and compulsion to escape. The thump of her own heart deafened her ears.

"Yes. My car. My house."

But— That wasn't possible. The sheer coincidence meant he would have known who she was before she got here. Was he a mind reader? Had he known what she planned even as they had made love? Then somehow tricked her into coming here?

No one had known what she had planned.

None of this made sense, but all she could blurt was, "*How*?"

An exhale of tested patience left him. "Come inside. We need to talk."

"No." She blipped the fob and moved to open the car door.

"I'm serious. Do not steal my car." He got both crutches under his arms and swooped fully into the garage, allowing the door to slam shut behind him.

They were in a standoff in the filtered light through the row of small windows across the top of the big doors. She might be able to leap into the car and lock it before he reached her, but then what? He could disable the front gate in the time it took her to pull out of the garage and get down the short driveway.

He must have calculated all of that himself. His posture eased slightly while his gaze flickered over her face and shoulders.

"How are you? You look good."

She doubted it and suddenly wished she looked like her old self, not a runaway from a punk rock band. Her brown hair with its faded blue ends hung around her face in air-dried frizz. She no longer owned makeup and her threadbare shorts and T-shirt had been second-hand when she had bought them from a Goodwill store six months ago.

"How—" Her throat kept going dry. He looked very disreputable and dangerous with his blackened eye and air of watchfulness. Murderous. "How did you get in? The security system is on."

"I came by boat and used my phone to disable it before I walked up." He drew his phone from his shorts pocket and tapped. His mouth twisted in a very poor imitation of a smile. "It's fully armed again now."

Meaning the garage doors would scream bloody murder if she opened one.

In the months of talking to herself without anyone around to be offended, she had developed quite a potty mouth and let one slip without thinking.

His brow went up. The corner of his mouth dug in with dark amusement. "I usually prefer some foreplay first, but I'm happy to accommodate if you're feeling an urgent need."

It wasn't funny. All of this was deeply distressing. Her veins were burning with adrenaline, her chest tight at being trapped. Then there was that other betraying part of her that was overjoyed to see him again. All those bunched muscles that had gathered her up, those sexy lips set between the carved hollows of his cheeks. He had kissed her *everywhere*. The hot light in his eyes seemed to recollect it as vividly as she did, freshly burning those kisses into her psyche.

She had spent *way* too much time replaying their night together. Often, in the dark of night and the privacy of her bed, she had let herself imagine they had had more between them than pheromones and a free evening.

In stark daylight, confronting him, she acknowledged that she had been played by a player. He had been way too good at sex to be anything less, and he had clearly been ten steps ahead of her the whole time.

"I thought this house belonged to a couple in divorce." Her voice wavered despite her best efforts to steady it. "The housekeeper—"

"Wanted time off. Her daughter was expecting."

She blinked as she absorbed that. "Okay, but how did you arrange for me to come here?" She already knew. The offer had been too good to be true and she'd fallen for it anyway. "*Why* did you? Oh, God, do you work for Troy?" Her stomach bottomed out.

"No." The smug amusement that had hovered around his mouth disappeared. "Your story broke a few days after we met." His jaw hardened and the curl in his mouth became very cynical. "Once it became clear you had disappeared, I made it my job to find you."

"*Why?*"

His brows winged up. "Why did you go into hiding?" The note of challenge in his tone suggested he knew the answer.

"Snitches get stitches." She tried to shrug it off, as if her knees weren't knocking with terror that she'd been located. And because it was true. People hated a tattletale. "A lot of rich, powerful people are either implicated or lost a chunk of their fortune." Maybe Everett was one of them? She hugged herself. "I don't imagine anyone is happy with me right now, but I can't afford a bodyguard. My only choice was to disappear." Even her last resort strategy offered no guarantee she would survive it.

"Don't forget the paparazzi," he said with mocking helpfulness. "There's a six-figure price on your headshot."

"You don't have to make it sound like a bounty!" Her skin was clammy. She couldn't even swallow, her throat was so dry and tight.

"That's what it is." He started to approach her.

She set one foot inside the car. If she jumped inside, she could get the door slammed and locked, hopefully pop out the other side before he had time to get around.

He only moved as far as the motorcycle, where it stood on its kickstand near a utility sink. He lowered to balance his weight against the tilted seat, releasing a small sigh as though relieved to take a load off.

It was a sneaky move, one that put him a lot closer to her and trapped her in the V of the open door. Rather than a whole car, now there was only the corner of the car's short trunk between them.

He could probably move a lot faster than he was letting on. She remembered *exactly* how powerful his legs had been, hard as sculpted oak between her own.

She looked away, not wanting him to guess what she was thinking. Feeling. Tendrils of yearning were unfurling in her belly. Her blood had become molasses, making her breaths heavy and her movements slow.

"You did a good job of covering your tracks." He sounded as if he admired her for it. "Took me over a week to find where you were staying."

"You found me in a *week*?" Her stomach cramped. She had tried so *hard* to disappear. It was demoralizing to have failed so quickly.

In the next second, she wondered what it meant that he had looked for her, but as quickly as her heart lifted, it dropped like a stone. If he had wanted to see her, he would have appeared a lot sooner than six months after their night together.

"I'm better at finding people than they are at getting lost." He spoke as if it was an absolute fact. *I'm taller than average. I bench press two-forty.*

The way he slouched on the motorcycle was like an old-time poster of a rebel hero with his stubble and bruises and pensive scowl. She'd never had a thing for that type. Not until right this moment. Why? It was self-destructive. Her mother had fallen for a bad boy and had been in hiding her whole life as a result. Bianca had stumbled into an engagement with a white-collar criminal, who had wanted to use her up then throw her to the wolves. Men with dark hearts were not worth the bother.

But all she could think about was Everett's mouth in the crook of her neck, his hands on her arms and the small of her back. His weight on her and his thickness moving powerfully within her, filling her with tension and intense waves of pleasure.

Was there a carbon monoxide leak in here? She couldn't catch her breath.

"When reward money climbs that high, landlords and employers grow tempted to line their own pockets. I had to draw you out and tuck you somewhere safe."

"I got the number from a flyer in a bodega! How could you know I would call it?"

"I didn't. It's a numbers game." He shrugged. "You didn't have any income sources that I could discern so I put in listings with all of the under-the-table outfits. Dog walking, childcare, computer work… Anything that might catch your interest. My criteria made me sound racist as hell and kind of a pervert, but it filtered out ninety percent of the applicants. Within a week, you turned up."

"You don't even have a dog," she noted with annoyance.

"I would have got one."

If only she'd known, she might have had company all this time.

"You found me, then went to all that trouble to get me here without speaking to me or letting me know?" Her mind was derailing all over again, trying to calculate how much time, effort and money he had put into that. "Why? Are you a private investigator or something?"

His mouth opened, shut, then, "Not anymore."

"What does *that* mean?"

"It means I'm off the clock. This is more of a hobby."

"A creepy one!"

"I gave you a job and a safe place to stay. You were free to leave anytime. It's not like I watched you on the cameras."

"Did you?" she screeched.

"No." He rolled his eyes as if she was the one being a weirdo.

"And I'm supposed to believe you," she scoffed.

"Whether you believe me or not is your choice. If you decide to leave, go forth with my blessing. Not with my car," he added, pointing a warning finger. "But walk away if that's what you want to do. Understand by doing so, however, that I will get what I want, and you won't get anything except a lot of attention, much of it negative. Dangerous, even."

She clenched her fist at her side, asking warily, "What do *you* want?"

"For you to come out of hiding." With a flat

smile, he waved at his state of injury. "I've been implicated in your disappearance, Bianca. My name must be cleared."

He'd been attacked because of her? She felt ill.

"How could *you* be implicated?"

"You left your luggage with the concierge at my hotel. Eventually, your... Have I got this right? Troy Ackerley is your fiancé?"

"Ex," she assured him, but a hollow feeling opened up behind her breastbone. She couldn't really see the color of his eyes in the low light, but she suspected they had turned frosty and forbidding. His voice sure had.

"I'm not sure he got that memo. He's still feeling very proprietary." Everett curled his lip. "His people were delivering a message as much as squeezing me for your whereabouts."

She clasped the edge of the car door so hard she should have bent the metal.

"Did you..." Her tongue felt as though it had swollen too big for her mouth and her head grew light.

She couldn't blame him for telling them where she was, but stark fear poured into her bloodstream, dampening her eyes. She looked to the wide garage door, mentally planning the route she would take to that *other* mansion if she was able to get out this gate. She was far more comfortable risking Everett's wrath by stealing his car than that of Troy if he caught up to her. She would definitely need protection if that happened.

"I'm not an amateur, Bianca," Everett said indignantly. "Of course, I didn't tell them where you are."

"Even though…" She looked to his bandaged knee. "Are you okay? Is it broken?"

"Swollen. I'll mend. The men who jumped me will be out of commission much longer."

He had fought them off. She shouldn't find that sexy. It wasn't. Violence was never a solution, but she was wavering in this space between worry for him and guilt that he'd been attacked because of her, yet he was brushing it off, confident that he had come out ahead. She couldn't help being affected by that.

"If they think you and I are involved, they'll come to your house," she noted, blood turning cold.

"All my houses are held by numbered companies. Ackerley's clown show took six months to draw a line from your abandoned luggage, through the hotel registry, to the fact we were on the same flight. I'm not worried about them finding us anytime soon, but they've become very annoying, trying to dig up dirt on me that doesn't exist. You and I need to plan how you'll come forward, so they'll get off my back."

Panicked at the mere thought, she vehemently shook her head. "I *can't* come forward."

CHAPTER TWO

SHE WAITED FOR him to argue, but Everett held his position in silence, as though there was no debate because in this case there wasn't. Plus, he found people filled a silence in a very revealing way if he let them.

Besides, it gave him the chance to take a long sip, drinking her in like fine brandy. Her lack of makeup only accentuated how lovingly her features had been crafted. And those lips. She was biting the bottom one, making him want to suck it. Again. He wanted to bite his own lip and groan out his six months of celibacy.

He wanted to touch her. Her shapeless T-shirt and low-slung cutoffs were sexier than any French lingerie, making his palms itch. Her braless breasts lifted the cotton off her tanned stomach providing a glimpse of her navel. Her golden-brown thighs were smooth and soft and went on for miles. All of her was like that. Endlessly, sensually pleasing. He'd spent way too many nights reliving exactly how hedonistic and generous and responsive she was.

Yet he had forgotten this effect she had on him, the one where desire dragged all his brain cells into a knot of craving in his groin. Actually, he had underestimated it, thinking he could control it the way he controlled most everything else, but this yank on his inner animal was even more potent than he recalled.

This was the reason he had let desire override his instincts, buying her dinner and sleeping with her against his better judgment.

No. He had to be honest with himself. He had relapsed and *embraced* the risk in seeing her. The nature and level of risk had been a mystery, which had been part of the appeal, but rather than heed the prickle down his spine, he had given in and scratched his itch, arrogantly certain he could weather any repercussions that came from their night together.

And this damned sexual heat had muffled the signals. When her voice had thinned, or her gaze had dropped, he'd seen it as a reaction to the brush of his foot against hers or the fact their stare had already been locked too long as a moment ripened with anticipation. She had licked her lips and stammered, but only in response to his most innocuous questions. *Should we order dessert? Are you cold?*

That last had been in response to how her nipples had stiffened beneath the silk of her blouse. Such a physical sign of arousal wasn't something she could fake, and she hadn't realized where his gaze had strayed when she answered, *Not at all.*

He'd been on fire himself, skating on an edge between fascination and caution, as though she was a tigress who could turn on him, but since he was close enough, he was compelled to reach out, pet and stroke.

She had captured all his attention, lighting up when she laughed and challenging his opinions and growing wistful as she talked about her future. *My work situation is complicated. I just broke my engagement, and he was my employer. I'm facing a life change.*

He had already done a cursory search and knew where she worked. There hadn't been a reason to linger on that dispiriting topic, so he'd ordered dessert. They'd shared it and held hands as they walked through the hotel grounds to the beach. They had kissed beneath the moonlight, her back shifting beneath his palms, hips tilting into his in a way that still heated his blood when he thought of it. He'd invited her upstairs and she had proceeded to reset his bar for one-night stands, making it impossible for him to settle for any of the pale imitations he'd been offered since.

Never once through all of that had she given

away the enormous step she had been about to take.

When her face and name had hit the headlines a few days later, he'd been surprised, yet not. He had waltzed into her minefield on his own two feet, but he'd been angry at himself, feeling foolish and wondering if he'd been taken in by a pro.

He couldn't imagine how, though. Nothing in her background suggested a history like his own, which had left him with an irritating amount of concern for her. She was a woman of limited resources pitting herself against a well-financed corruption machine. His conscience had compelled him to help her even though he had left the dark underworld of espionage so he wouldn't be responsible for other people's lives anymore.

Ensconcing her here had been his compromise. He'd stayed in New York, keeping half the Eastern Seaboard between them, digging into the Morris and Ackerley charges to better understand it. To help.

Because she'd haunted his thoughts no matter how hard he tried to dismiss her.

Then, yesterday, he'd been dragged into an alley and found himself fighting for his life. And hers. That's what had given him the strength to put those men on the ground. Everett had been terrified for Bianca. He hadn't breathed easy until he'd seen for himself that she was safe.

Which didn't make sense. How could he care so much what happened to a woman he'd slept with *once*? Okay, they'd made love three times, but he barely knew her. And she'd pulled him into a rat's nest of trouble, one to which he was rapidly becoming an accomplice. That peeved him deeply.

Worse, she was causing him to backslide into unraveling conspiracies and protecting sources. It wouldn't do. He'd made promises to his mother. To himself.

Now that he knew she was unharmed, he would insist she clear his name, put some distance between them, and he would never see her again.

His stomach reflexively clenched in resistance, but he ignored it.

"Could I..." She finally broke, folding her arms and hunched her shoulders defensively. "Press releases are my forte." Her head came up. "I could issue a statement, make it clear that I don't really know you." Her expression was sincere, as if that was a genuinely helpful suggestion.

He snorted.

"It's *true*," she said defensively, but her cheeks stained a darker pink. The way her chin dipped and her lips rolled in suggested she was recalling exactly how well acquainted they were.

That was gratifying, at least. If he was still hostage to this pull between them, at least he had a cellmate.

She tucked her jaw-length hair behind her ear, and even the fact it was rich brunette at the roots and distressed as old denim on the ends was sexy as hell.

He absently closed his empty hand, recalling the satisfying give of those thick, springy waves between his fingers. It was a lot shorter now, but he bet it still smelled of almonds and citrus. He wanted to pick it up and set his mouth in the hollow at the base of her skull, feeling her squirm, and push her bottom into his groin in response.

So damned stupid. He gave his head a shake to dispel the fantasy.

"I'm not dismissing the idea because we know each other in the biblical sense." There had been nothing puritanical about that night. It had been delightfully debauched. "It's a very naive offer from someone who struck me as intelligent. Have you not seen the news?"

"Not lately." Her mouth twisted. "I stopped watching. It was too depressing."

No doubt. Still, "You haven't happened across any headlines?"

"I don't go online. I was afraid of leaving digital footprints. I even put tape over the camera on the computer." She chucked her chin toward the door to the kitchen, then sent him a baleful look. "I didn't think of the security cameras, or I would have covered them, too."

"I didn't even peek at you today." He had reviewed the map of sensors to see which house doors were open, surmising from there that she was in the kitchen. Then he had disabled all the cameras so he wouldn't activate them as he entered.

"Look, Morris and Ackerley are pretending all is well, but they're imploding. Their legal bills are mounting, and anyone who was able to pull their money out of the company already has. Their assets are frozen, employees haven't been paid, more victims are coming forward and most are going to the press with their complaints. The fact that the whistleblower is missing is stirring up swarms of hashtags. Your fiancé—"

"*Ex*," she reminded, teeth clamped on a nip of her cuticle while her fixed gaze impelled him to keep talking.

"Ackerley suddenly realized he could be on the hook for murder charges if you don't turn up alive. He doesn't know that I'm helping you, but he doesn't care. Now that he's figured out I was the last person to see you, he has issued an ultimatum. Either I tell him where you are or take the fall for your absence. It would make a nice distraction for him to sic the media and authorities onto me, and it would be highly inconvenient for me. Therefore, you have to reappear, make it clear I had nothing to do with your decision to expose them and draw the fire back where it belongs."

"I'm really sorry." Her tone held the placating tone of, *I'd like to help you, but I can't.* "I wasn't trying to set you up for anything like this."

"No? Why did you sleep with me then?" Because, as she'd briefly evaded him with skills he usually only saw in a fellow operative, he had begun to suspect ulterior motives in her spending those erotic hours with him. Had she meant to entrap him?

She looked away, hugging herself as she flushed with embarrassment, mouth pinched with reluctance to speak.

"Because you made it sound as though you'd recently broken your engagement and wanted to move on, yet you were still engaged." Everett didn't know why he was so outraged by that. When he'd brought her to his room, he hadn't planned to see her again. He sure as hell hadn't expected to feel this roil of indignation if he did, especially one stained with such a dark green of possessiveness. But spiky barbs of jealousy sat sharply under his skin.

"I did want to move on. I was angry with Troy, but that wasn't why I—" She cleared her throat before admitting in a strangled voice, "I was attracted to you."

He wanted to cage her face in his palms and look into her eyes. He wanted to get right up against her to learn if this thing between them had been as real as it had seemed, but he kept his distance. His focus.

"That's the only reason you slept with me? Attraction? You weren't deliberately drawing me into your plot?"

"What? No." Her eyes flashed wide with shock. "Why would I?"

Why indeed? It wasn't as if he had a secret past that she might have discovered and thought she could weaponize.

She held his gaze, earnest tension sitting across her cheekbones.

"I knew I shouldn't have dinner with you." Her voice was tight with mortification. "I was planning to land, send my files and disappear, but when you asked me to dinner..." She showed him a pensive profile. "I was anxious to get away from Troy and everything else, but I was scared." Her hands were flexing in remembered anxiety. "I wasn't sure how to get rid of my luggage, but I realized that if I met you for dinner, I could leave it at your hotel as an insurance policy. If I chickened out on sending the files, I could pick up my bag and my life in the morning. If I went through with it, it would take the concierge some time to wonder why I hadn't come back for it."

Smart. And it rang true. "But you spent the night."

"That wasn't part of my plan. Truly. I don't sleep with men I don't know or like or, you know, want to sleep with." She was blushing again.

He took a similar approach with his intimate partners, but had to ask, "Does that mean you were sleeping with your fiancé or not?"

"I wasn't." She shook her head in an urgent reassurance, as if it mattered as much to her as it did to him. "I was desperate to break the engagement, but if I had, he might have realized I was about to set fire to his great-grandfather's firm so I made excuses for why I couldn't spend the night with him."

"Headache?" he guessed dryly.

She grimaced and her shoulders came up to her ears. "I claimed so many migraines, he booked me for an MRI."

He refused to laugh, but a gust of relief left his lungs. This was what had transfixed him that evening. There was no chance for boredom when everything about her was unexpected. She veered effortlessly from introspective to playful, from sincere to sarcastic, then dipped to warm and sensual as her expression softened. A rueful smile touched her lips.

"Why did you get engaged in the first place?" It was the last question he should be asking, but he wanted to know. "Did you love him?"

"No. Not really. It just sort of happened." She wrinkled her nose as though she still suffered regret. "When he hired me after I interned, I was really flattered. And yes, I realize my credentials were less a factor in my landing that job than the fact I fit the image they wanted to project." She rolled her eyes.

No false modesty. She knew she was beautiful, knew it was an advantage, but didn't wield it like a weapon. He liked that about her, too.

Focus, fool.

"Troy took a personal interest in my professional development. He kept giving me more responsibility and shifting me into different departments. My specialty is marketing, but my degree is business, so I thought I was elevating my skill set. Eventually I realized I was doing his work so he didn't have to, but Mom was sick, and when she passed, he was really kind. He sent flowers and said my absence had made him realize I deserved a raise. Looking back, I see he was making sure he didn't lose my 'elevated skill set.'" She made air quotes. "But it felt good to be taken out for fancy dinners when I was feeling so blue."

"It felt good to be taken advantage of when

you were vulnerable?" He had nothing but contempt for men like that.

"I didn't see it, but yes, that's what he was doing. By the time I was plotting my escape, I was certain he had been keeping at least one woman on the side the whole time he was romancing me, but it felt genuine. I wasn't thinking it would lead to marriage, though. Not until he took me into a corner office and said, 'This can be yours if you say yes.'"

"And went down on one knee? What a tool." He was so embarrassed by his own sex sometimes.

"Right? But considering how hard I'd been working I didn't see it as nepotism or even a condition of our engagement. I had earned that promotion. He told me I had. He said he didn't want to lose me to another firm *or* another man. I thought all these big gestures meant he loved me. My mom was gone, and I wanted a family one day. He seemed like a caring man who was a good provider. I thought grief was holding me back from deep feelings and decided, why *not* him?"

"Then you realized why not," Everett deduced grimly.

"I did," she said somberly. "I came across some transactions that I had done for him and… Basically, they were stealing. He was getting me to do his work so he could keep his own hands clean."

"Plausible deniability."

"Exactly. He wanted me to take the blame if it came to light. Which is why I had to expose it." She took hold of the open door of the car, wavered as though trying to decide whether to get in or close it. "It feels good to talk about it. *To talk.* To a human. But be honest." She sent him a look of consternation. "Are you here to find out how much I really know? Or, like, hang me out to dry in some way?"

"I'm not an assassin, if that's what you're implying," he said dryly. "I'm not a cop or a reporter, either."

"What, then? What are you 'not anymore?'" she amended, eyes narrowing as she recollected his earlier remark.

"We'll save that for another time." Like never.

"But I'm supposed to trust you?" She tsked and shut the car door, coming to the back of the car, where she leaned her hip next to the taillight.

He tried not to wince. The paintwork could be buffed.

"Is there a reason you don't want to trust me?" he asked.

"Aside from the fact that you tricked me into staying here?"

"Where you've been very safe and comfortable," he pointed out.

"It's suspicious, though. What do you get out of it?" She crossed her arms and tilted her head.

"A housekeeper. And the knowledge I did a good deed." It had been so much more complex than that, but he rose and tucked his crutches beneath his arm, having learned that standing was a great way to close a topic and take command of pretty much anything.

Her solemn gaze met his black eye. "If ending up on crutches is what happens to someone who knows where I am, what will they do to *me* if I come out of hiding?"

His heart lurched.

"Nothing." He swallowed the ashes that came into his mouth. "I'll arrange protection. Security, a lawyer, a PR agent, a safe place to stay. Anything and everything you need."

"Why? Do you have a grudge against Morris and Ackerley? Were you an investor?"

"No."

"This is just to keep your name out of it?"

"Yes."

"It's that important to you."

Obviously.

"What happens when someone realizes you've paid for all of those things?"

"They won't."

"Who will they think paid for it?" she asked

with exasperation. "The woman who claims she didn't have anything to do with defrauding all those people of millions of dollars?" She pointed at herself.

"I have work-arounds." He shrugged that off. "How do you feel about a six-figure book deal? If you don't want to write it, I can hire a ghost writer."

"Where does *that* money come from?" Her hands went up in bafflement. "Are you a drug dealer? Arms? What?"

"No." Good guesses, though. "Are you always this suspicious?"

"I just want to know what's going on! You're such a good Samaritan, you want to give me a six-figure book deal to hide the fact that you've been helping me. Heck, you hid that information from *me*. Why? Oh, God." Horror washed across her expression. "You're not married, are you?"

"No." If he wasn't so aggravated with her, he would revel in the way she looked ill at the thought of him being committed to someone else. "When you started making headlines, I realized our night could surface and bite me, so I tucked you out of sight. That's all."

"So this was *never* about protecting me and always about protecting *you*?"

So smart and so maddening. "Yes."

Barbed hurt flashed in her eyes, causing a pinch behind his heart.

"You've gone to a lot of trouble and expense to keep our night hidden." She tossed her head. "It's not like I was ever going to tell anyone that we hooked up. It was a onetime thing that didn't mean anything to me, either. That's why I left as soon as you were asleep."

"I wasn't asleep."

Her head snapped around, appalled hurt flashing in her wide eyes.

He bit back a curse, annoyed with himself. He hadn't liked hearing their night meant nothing and had struck back.

"Thanks, but no thanks," she said frostily, pushing off the car and starting toward the door to the house. "I'll take Option B, the one where I take my chances with the paparazzi and my fiancé."

"Bianca!" He moved so fast lurching to catch her arm, he dropped a crutch, stupid damned things.

She yanked free of his touch and whirled to confront him.

"I wasn't ashamed of being so easy that night until right now, when you made me feel like I curdle your image like sour milk. You shouldn't have asked me to dinner if you're embarrassed to be associated with me. Did you think of that? And don't tell me to trust you! You could be leading Troy to me right now for all I know."

Ah hell, she was shaking. Scared.

A cool space opened behind his breastbone. She wouldn't be this close to falling apart if she had some master plan in place. She was flying by the seat of her pants and was running out of fuel.

"I'm not embarrassed we slept together," he said quietly. "My life is very complicated—"

"Really? What's that like?"

He licked his lips, still enamored with that snappy wit of hers, but it struck him how hard these months must have been for her. In the past, when he left someone in a safe house, they had caretakers and he visited as often as he could, keeping their spirits up.

"I had the means to help you and I wanted to. I still do." *Don't get further involved*, the nagging voice in his head reminded. *Clear your name, get her out of your house, never see her again.*

She rejected his offer with a lost shake of her head, blinking and pressing her lips flat to hide their trembling.

"Bianca," he chided. Pure instinct had him holding out an arm. "Come here. You don't have to do this all by yourself. That's why I'm here."

Fool, that voice said, but when she gave a sniff and looked so damned slight and vulnerable, he couldn't take it. He stepped closer and nudged the back of her arm.

A sob left her and she turned herself into his

chest. Her arms went around his waist, hugging tight. She hunched close as though sheltering from the elements and a small shudder went through her.

The impact on him was cataclysmic.

He had thought about her constantly, wanting the feel of her narrow back under his hand and the tickle of her hair under his chin. He smoothed her spine, saying nothing while she took unsteady breaths, trying to keep a grip on her composure.

"You're still very safe," he assured her. "We're only talking about what might happen. Nothing has changed. Not yet."

"I kept thinking about you." She drew back enough to look up at him. Her lashes were spiky with unshed tears. "I wished I had been honest with you. That I had given you my side before I turned up on the news. It's like a hallucination that you're even here. That I've been in your house all this time. I want to trust you, Everett. I do. But I don't know if I can."

Same, he almost said, but his senses were taking in her perfume of oranges and sunshine. He liked the press of her curves against his chest and abdomen and thighs. She was a puzzle piece that fit exactly into the landscape of his own shape, blending heat and sensation, filling his vision with color, blurring the space between them into nothing.

The atmosphere shifted. Her searching gaze drifted to his mouth. She swallowed.

They each nudged their feet a fraction closer, bodies leaning more firmly into one another.

Careful, Everett. Not in a million years would he make a move on a woman who was only seeking comfort, but as he drew a breath and started to pull back, the light in her eyes dimmed. Her beautiful mouth, which was *right there*, trembled with rejection. She firmed it and her chin crinkled. Her weight shifted away from his.

His arm instinctually tightened, trying to keep her from dissolving like loose sand through his fingertips.

Her gaze flashed up to his and, damn it, he'd been thinking of kissing her again for *so long*.

As he slowly, slowly let his head lower, she stayed right where she was. In fact, her body inclined more into his, melting and receptive, warm and welcoming.

He touched his mouth to hers and a tingling dance slid across his lips. Smooth, plump flesh gave way as he settled deeper into their kiss. A soft noise throbbed in her throat, one that added to the moans and sobs and cries of ecstasy that echoed in his erotic dreams.

There was a worth-the-wait quality to this kiss, but he groaned thinking that he had known where she was all this time and could have had a thousand of these kisses by now. He shouldn't have wasted any of that time. She opened her mouth further and he drew her closer, sliding his arm around her as he rocked his mouth to deepen their kiss.

He became so lost in her scent and taste, he didn't immediately catch the flavor on her tongue or the faint aroma clinging to the hand she raised to touch his cheek, not until his lips began to burn.

His lips began to burn.

He grabbed hold of her upper arms and set her back a step.

"How did you know?" he growled.

True fear sent his heart slamming with the force of a wrecking ball, nearly cracking his ribs. The prickling sensation was already spreading into his mouth and down his throat.

A clock began ticking in his head. He would never make it to the boat. Was there a first aid kit in the house? Why hadn't he grabbed his pen? He always had one in his pocket, but he'd been fiddling with the security system on his phone and too impatient to see her. *Idiot.*

"How did I know what?" she asked as he swiveled away and hopped with one crutch toward the door to the kitchen.

"That I'm allergic to peanuts."

This time it might actually kill him.

CHAPTER THREE

"Is it severe?" Bianca rushed ahead of him to hold the door, afraid to touch him again. "Do you have a pen? There's a first aid kit in the laundry room."

Her mind raced. She'd had a classmate in middle school who had had a deadly allergy to bee stings. The whole class had learned how to administer the epinephrine, but she had never actually jabbed anyone. She didn't even know if there was a pen here.

Everett began to wheeze and grasped at the doorframe. He was likely winded by hopping on one crutch as his windpipe closed. Behind the determination in his eyes was angry despair.

Reacting purely on instinct, she slapped her hand across the garage door buttons.

As she had suspected, the moment they began grinding upward, the security system bleated its alarm.

Everett flashed her a look of disbelief.

"You need help." She didn't let herself think

of what might happen after. "The ambulance can reach you fastest if you stay out here. Lie down before you fall down." She grasped his arm because he was already sinking to the floor.

As he crumpled to the concrete, she released him and ran inside to look for a pen. She would make one if she had to.

Over hidden speakers, a woman's voice identified herself as working for TecSec, the security company. "All cameras are activated. Your movements are being recorded."

"We have a medical emergency. Anaphylaxis. Order an ambulance *now*." Bianca banged through the cupboards in the laundry room and grabbed the red kit with the white cross. She dumped it unceremoniously onto the top of the washer. Bandages and scissors and antiseptic… Where was the damned pen?

"An ambulance has been dispatched," the voice said calmly. "It should arrive in four minutes. The gate will open when it nears. Our notes indicate there is a stock of self-injectable epinephrine in the master bedroom. Emergency personnel are asking if this is an insect bite—"

"Peanut allergy." Bianca leaped up the stairs two at a time, tearing down the hall and into the master bathroom where she quickly found a box of two needles. "For God's sake, cut that siren. It's killing my ears," she shouted as she raced back to the garage.

The noise silenced and the disembodied voice began reading instructions on how to administer the needle, reminding her to check the date.

Everett was on his back on the concrete floor, one arm thrown over his eyes. His lips were blue, his chest shaking as he strained to breath. He lifted his arm as she appeared. The tense resignation in his expression flickered to surprise.

"Nice opinion you have of me," she muttered, fumbling to scrabble the needle from the box. The date was fine, thank God.

She pulled the ends off and lifted the edge of his shorts so she could press the red end against the outside of his thigh. He didn't flinch at the sting of the needle going in, only held her stare while a hazy curtain seemed to descend over the shimmering blue of his eyes.

"Don't you dare, Everett." She finished counting as she held it against his skin, then covered the needle and set it aside, rubbing the spot on his leg with her other hand.

She was about to ask the disembodied voice if she should give him another, but she heard the ambulance siren approaching. The gate was rattling open.

She started to cup Everett's face, wanting to rouse him and see if he was just closing his eyes or actually falling unconscious, but she remembered she hadn't washed her hands.

The soap at the utility sink was an industrial grease remover, but she used it anyway, hurrying to wash her hands to her elbows and all over her face, rinsing her mouth and spitting, then using the nearby paper towel before discarding it.

As she came back to check Everett's pulse— he had one, but it was faint and very fast—the ambulance stopped in the cobblestoned forecourt. She waved and called out, then stepped back as one of the attendants ran up to crouch next to Everett, checking his vital signs.

Beyond the gate a dog walker paused to peer at their commotion.

Run, a voice of self-preservation urged her. *This is your last chance.*

Bianca looked to the other paramedic, who was bringing oxygen, then to Everett's limp form. She couldn't leave him like this, not when she was responsible for putting him in that state.

She hovered tensely, worried at how swift and grave they were being about packaging him for transport.

"Are you coming in the ambulance or—" The paramedic glanced at the sports car.

"I'm coming." She was in no fit state to drive. "Security, alarm the house as we leave."

"Of course. TecSec is pleased we could be of service today. A full report will be issued shortly."

She should have stayed at the house to clean it, Bianca thought several times over the next hours. Everett couldn't go back there until all traces of peanuts were gone.

If he went back there.

The EMTs had been forced to insert a tube into his windpipe to ensure he was receiving enough oxygen. Twice they had thought they would have to administer CPR.

When they arrived at the hospital, someone asked if she was his wife and Bianca had unhesitatingly said, "Yes." She had signed every piece of paper they put in front of her.

A short while ago, they had decided his blood pressure was strong enough and the swelling in his airway reduced enough, that they had removed his air tube. Now he only had a tube resting in his nostrils, continuing to provide extra oxygen. He was still hooked up to IV and a number of monitors. He was still unconscious.

As she sat curled in a chair beside his bed, she kept trying to think of herself and her situation, trying to work out the best course of action for *her*, but her mind wouldn't cooperate. It wouldn't even stick to all that had happened this morning and the revelation that he had been her employer all this time.

No, her brain insisted on conjuring memories of their night together, the way it had for months, lingering over the slow seduction of a dinner and strolling the boardwalk, the night air caressing her shoulders and arms, then his light touch following those same paths. A kiss that had drawn her so far from this world, she had felt drugged when he had lifted his head and said, "Come to my room."

It had been both invitation and command. She'd been incapable of resisting either.

She hadn't known lovemaking like that was possible. For her, sex had always been a pleasant if tame and awkward encounter. She knew men thought she was attractive, but they'd always looked at her like a prize, making her feel removed, as though she was being made love *to*, not *with*.

Everett had definitely ensured she was with him every step of the way. He had been in no hurry and he had brushed her hair behind her shoulder and said, "Your hair is beautiful. It smells like you," he added. "Run it across me. I want your scent all over me."

He had touched and kissed her everywhere, along the base of her neck and down her back, inside her elbow and even her ankle. "Your skin is so soft. Do you like this? Move my hand.

Show me what makes you feel good." Instead of telling her what he wanted her to do to him, he had asked, "Do you want my mouth here? Do you need me to do this harder?"

She had grown emboldened with her own caresses, doing things she'd never done, rubbing her breasts on his erection and licking her way down his body purely to hear him groan with tortured anticipation.

Time had stopped as she became immersed in the experience, each caress so sharply exquisite it nearly hurt. Twice he had brought her to the brink and backed off, continuing to pleasure her in a slower, more indirect way, keeping her on that plateau of heightened arousal while building them toward even grander pinnacles.

When he had finally thrust into her, she had nearly wept at how badly she had needed his penetration. All inhibitions had been abandoned by then. She was completely his, reveling in his slow, deep, powerful strokes. She had moaned her encouragement without any sense of decorum or restraint. She'd said filthy things, telling him what she wanted. *Needed.* More. Harder.

Still he had made it last, rolling them across the bed, encouraging her to ride him, then pinning her beneath him again, determined to wring every last sensation from every stroke.

When the tantalizing stars of orgasm had begun to coalesce behind her eyes, when her breath shortened and her body was one live nerve, he had done exactly what she needed and given her more. Harder.

She had shattered. The crashing waves of orgasm had shot all the way into her fingers and toes. Through the storm, as her body ceased to belong to her and her consciousness was devolved to its most primitive form, she had felt him pulsing within her. Shuddering upon her, skin adhered to hers. He had released jagged noises with his hot breath against her ear, matching her unintelligible cries of ecstasy with his own.

They had been together. United. For the first time in her life, she had felt as though she was truly connected to another person. Broken down to her most basic level, but unbreakable because she had him. They were one.

Then he'd done it again. And once more after they'd dozed.

As the sky had turned pearlescent, she had made herself rise. It had been harder than all the planning and plotting she'd done to leave the man she had been engaged to, but she'd left, aware pieces of herself would stay with Everett, but she was leaving everything behind, and she was deeply glad he held *those* pieces.

Then.

Now she knew he had feigned sleep and let her go.

Had he been relieved by her departure?

My life is very complicated.

She had hated him for a minute there. She had hated herself. Their night had become tawdry, and she had felt cheap.

Then he had hugged her. *You don't have to do this all by yourself anymore.*

Those words, the way he'd held her... Profound relief had nearly buckled her knees. His promise to stand by her had been everything she had dreamed of while she'd been rattling around in that empty house, wishing she knew what came next. Had it been a rescue fantasy? Perhaps. But he was the man she had wanted to rescue her this whole time and here he was.

Then she had nearly killed him.

She sat at his bedside, earning double takes from nurses and other hospital personnel as they recognized her. She didn't have so much as a spare coin in her pocket for a phone call and only one person to call if she did. Would her father even take her call? Believe her? Welcome her? Or reject her?

If she possessed one ounce of self-preservation, she would leave before Everett woke, but until he woke, she couldn't seem to make herself leave this chair, let alone his room or the hospital. She needed to know he would be okay.

She desperately hoped he wouldn't hate her.

"Hello." A male voice forced her to drag her gaze off Everett and glance to the door.

A very handsome man of thirty-something had appeared in the open doorway. He was in a wheelchair, but not one of the hospital ones. It was streamlined and clearly custom made for him, given he showed no sign of illness and wore stylish linen trousers draped over the ends of his amputated legs. His shirt was a collared polo in a berry brown that clung to his extremely well-built chest and biceps as he smoothly rolled in.

Her next thought was that he possessed an air of confidence similar to the one Everett exuded, especially when the man casually leaned down and released the doorstop, letting the door fall closed behind him as he came up to the bed.

His face hardened as he took in Everett's black eye and bandaged hands.

"That's not a peanut reaction. What happened?" The way his hardened glare turned on her and pinned her through the heart had her pressing into her chair.

"He showed up like that." She scratched her neck, not sure how much to say. She had told the doctor the peanut contact had been the fault of a gardener because who would believe the man's wife didn't know about his allergy? Then she had quietly washed again with antiseptic wipes *and* brushed her teeth with a toothbrush that would likely be added to Everett's bill.

She instinctively knew not to lie to this man, though.

"I ate some peanut butter, then kissed him," she admitted in a mumble.

"On purpose?" The deadly way his voice dropped sent icicles jabbing into her plummeting stomach.

"*No.* I mean, it was consensual. *He* kissed *me*, if you want to be technical about it." She rubbed her clammy palms on her bare arms. "I didn't know about his allergy, or I never would have brought anything like that into his house."

He gave a snort of mild disgust and came around the end of the bed, so they weren't speaking over Everett's unconscious body.

"He only told me about it a year ago and downplayed how bad it was."

"And you are?" she prompted.

"Giovanni Catalano." He offered his hand. "A friend of Everett's, which makes me wonder why I wasn't invited to your wedding. Bianca."

"Um…" She had started to offer her name and hold out her hand, but she was so disconcerted, her fingers turned to limp celery as he closed his strong grip over them.

He was gentle, though. Brief.

"That's what they told me at admin. That his wife was with him." And he knew who she was.

His delving gaze was trying to put together how his friend had wound up married to the Morris and Ackerley whistleblower.

"I only said that so I could sign the papers for his care." It belatedly occurred to her that he might be a reporter or investigator. She set her feet on the floor and rose, feeling as though she was peeling off her own skin as she said, "But I guess if you're here to speak for him, I can leave." She didn't want to leave him, though. And she had nowhere to go.

Giovanni made the smallest adjustment to the angle of his wheelchair, but it was a very loud, *Thou shalt not pass*.

She lifted her brows, cornered between the bed and the window, but not afraid to vault over the hospital bed and the man she had put in it, if that's what it took to maintain her freedom.

"Someone has tipped off the press that you're here," Giovanni said. "You won't get out without help."

That wasn't much of a surprise. She was tempted to peek through the blinds but decided she'd better not. She sank back into the chair.

"Are you offering to help? Why?"

"I'm Everett's friend." He shot another look at the man that held shades of impatience and exasperation. "Thankfully, you've laid the groundwork. It's an easy spin to say you kept your marriage a secret to avoid media attention. We'll issue a statement that doesn't mention the allergy. A Jet Ski accident," he decided. "To account for his injuries. I'll order a change of clothes, so you'll be camera-ready when we walk to the car. We'll leave the minute he's awake and able to walk."

"And go *where*?" She had so many questions, she was tripping over her own tongue. "You can't just come in here and take control."

"Someone has to. I need to make some calls. Stay put." He neatly spun his chair.

Panicked belligerence had her saying, "I will not."

"Bianca," a voice rasped from the bed. "Do as you're told."

"I thought you retired," Giovanni said.

"I thought you did," Everett grumbled back.

He felt as though he'd been thrown down a flight of stairs and turned inside out. He sat on a lounger in the shade, his only true friend seated beside him. Bianca and Giovanni's wife, Freja, were in the far end of the pool catching the couple's twins as they jumped off the ledge into the water.

Bianca laughed as she was splashed by the energetic two-year-olds, her mood a complete one-eighty from how sullen she'd been in the SUV as they had left the hospital. She'd pulled on a simple wrap dress and chic sandals, coiled her blue-tipped hair under a floppy-brimmed hat and covered her eyes with huge black sunglasses. The bold red on her lips had emphasized her mouth's downward curve. She had used Everett's limping body as a shield as they passed the gathered photographers.

They had arrived to a cleaning crew wiping every wall and surface of his mansion. Everett had messaged his housekeeper from the hospital, and she had hurried in a service. She was quick to ask Bianca where the workers should make extra effort to remove traces of peanut butter. Then, because the twins had been begging to go in the pool, Bianca had been commandeered by Freja.

"Why are you even here?" Everett heard how ungrateful he sounded, but he could barely face the man as it was. Giovanni had done him a huge favor when he ought to have cut Everett out of his life completely by now.

"Our good friend at TecSec thought I might be interested in the security video that had just come across his desk. He was prepared to fly in himself, but I was closer. We were in New York, preparing to come for Freja's premiere this weekend. We moved up our trip and here we are."

"I meant why did you bother?" Everett said, but Giovanni was speaking over him.

"Was your reaction this dangerous when you ate those peanuts—"

"What's done is done," Everett cut in, not wanting to talk about the time he had deliberately ingested peanuts to clear his conscience where Freja was concerned. It had done nothing to square things with the man beside him.

Giovanni sighed. Annoyed. "It wasn't your fault, Everett. I wish you'd get over it and accept a dinner invitation now and again."

It *was* his fault, though. He and Giovanni had been friends in their school years, when Giovanni had kept him sane through a very dark time. Years later, Everett had recruited his friend into the spy game. They'd been a sort of dream team, but Everett hadn't forced Giovanni to stand down when he had known Giovanni was not at his mental best. His best friend had nearly been killed and it still turned his guts to gravel.

He loathed himself for endangering his friend and couldn't understand why Giovanni didn't.

"Freja never would have asked you to risk your life for her," Giovanni said quietly. "But thank you. What you did means the world to her."

"Don't get maudlin." Everett couldn't take it right now. Ever, really. "And don't expect me to thank you for your assistance today." He waved toward the pool. "I don't *want* a wife."

"Don't knock it till you try it."

Everett shot him a glower, but Giovanni only grinned, then chucked his chin.

"Seriously, are you working again?" he asked in an undertone.

"No."

"Then what are you doing with her?" Giovanni looked to Bianca.

"We crossed paths. She needed help. My involvement would have stayed between the two of us except…" He swirled a hand to encompass the farce of a day this had turned into.

"Judging by that pretty black-and-blue eye shadow you're wearing, it's not just between the two of you. If it's that dangerous, should you *stay* involved if you lack backup?"

This was why Everett had wanted to keep Giovanni on the payroll as long as possible. He never missed a thing and always drilled straight to the heart of a problem.

"What's my alternative? Leave her to face it alone? I'm in it now." According to the headlines, he was married to it.

"But can you trust her? After today?"

"She didn't know." And she had saved him.

An emotive vibration hit his sternum as he recalled that harrowing moment when Bianca had run into the house, leaving him collapsing on the garage floor.

He'd been furious at her for catching him off guard *again*, but it served him right. He had known she was dangerous from the get-go. Even when he learned how much trouble she was in, he had waded right in. He had spooked her with his surprise arrival and even though she had tripped the alarm, he had fully expected her to save herself, leaving him to take his chances on the ambulance arriving in time.

Part of him had wanted her to get herself into the clear, but in the twilight of fighting for enough oxygen, he'd been worried about her. Who would look out for her if he wasn't there to do it?

She had reappeared then, breathless, and jabbed him without any squeamishness. Her eyes had been shiny with fear, her mouth tight with determination.

Everything had fogged after that. He'd come back to Giovanni's voice, which hadn't been much of a surprise. Everett was a terrible friend, but Giovanni was a good one.

Everett might have let himself sink back into unconsciousness, safe in good hands, but Bianca's voice had pulled him back to wakefulness. He hadn't expected her to be there. That meant she had broken her cover. For him.

"Okay, but if you need anything—"

"I won't," Everett said flatly. "Stay out of it."

"*Dio, sei testardo,*" Giovanni muttered in Italian, calling Everett stubborn.

There was a pulse of silence where only the

splashes and squeals of the children sounded, then Giovanni continued in Italian.

"Fine, but this doesn't add up. Why did she stay in Miami?"

"Because I gave her the means," Everett replied, also using Italian.

"Why did she want to, though? She could have hopped a yacht, got work on a cruise ship… Why did she stay where her fiancé sent her?"

Everett had wondered those things, too. While he'd been apart from her, he had focused on looking into her employer's background to bolster the case against them, only running a cursory background check on Bianca.

She had been born in New York, her mother had been a nurse and Bianca had been an exemplary student. Her CV had checked out as had the grandmother in Miami leaving her money— although the timing had been off with that. The probate had finalized two years before Everett had met her. Beyond that, there hadn't been anything untoward.

"Finito?" Giovanni smiled as Freja and Bianca approached. "I'll help get them changed." He reached for his wheelchair.

Bianca cradled one of the towel-wrapped toddlers. The girl's lips were blue and her teeth were chattering. Bianca wore a white T-shirt over her bikini, the wet cotton plastered to her hips and upper thighs. Neon green showed through and beneath the hem, and her honey-gold thighs were sparkling with dripping water.

She's doing it again. Giovanni had just given Everett good reason to question her motives, but all Everett wanted to do was lick each of those drops off her skin.

"We should get to the hotel," Freja was saying to Giovanni. "Unless you two need more time?" She glanced to Everett with a glimmer of optimism.

"We're finished talking," Everett said crisply.

Giovanni settled into his chair and exchanged one of those married people looks with Freja, the kind that communicated a dozen thoughts at once. Everett couldn't interpret all of it, but he caught the part where Freja's mouth pressed flat with empathy.

Did she not realize Everett didn't deserve their forgiveness? He was poison. She ought to know that better than anyone.

"I didn't realize you weren't staying here," Bianca said with a wary flicker of her glance at Everett as she stooped to hand Louisa to Giovanni.

"We have such an entourage—it's best if we pay people to put up with us," Freja joked.

And this house wasn't really set up for Giovanni. Most of Everett's homes had at least the ground floor remodeled to accommodate his friend's chair, but Everett hadn't got around to making those changes here, which made him feel like an even bigger jerk.

"Lars is with us," Giovanni said, mentioning his physiotherapist. "Do you want me to send him over to look at your knee? Give you some exercises?"

"I'm fine." *Quit being nice*, Everett told him with a glare.

You could try it, Giovanni told him with a cocked brow.

"Oh! I had tickets set aside for you, for the premiere," Freja said to Everett. "That was before…" She rocked her head. "Today. But you hadn't seen it yet so I thought you might…"

She trailed off as she took in his stonewalling expression.

"No pressure. Whatever you decide. Yes, I know you're hungry." Freja nuzzled her nose against Theresa's as the little girl whispered an entreaty. "We're going to dry you two off and get you a snack for the drive to the hotel. Then we'll have a nice big dinner. Thank you so much for your help today," Freja said to Bianca. "I'll leave my number. Let's stay in touch."

"Oh. Yes. Thanks. It was my pleasure. Truly." Her smile faded as the couple retreated into the house. Bianca hugged herself against the chill of her dripping T-shirt. "Those girls are adorable and she's so nice. I didn't have the heart to tell her I don't even have a phone." The spark of wry humor in her eyes winked out as she met his eyes.

Everett was fighting to keep his gaze above the way her breasts swelled against the translucent fabric of her shirt.

It was a fair question. Why *had* she stayed in Miami?

"Well, I guess I'll, um, go change." She turned toward the cabanas.

"Your things are in my room. I had the housekeeper move them."

"Why?" She blinked her wet lashes in astonishment.

"Because we're married," he reminded pithily.

CHAPTER FOUR

BIANCA FINISHED REMOVING the lipstick that had smudged in the pool and stared at her clean face, almost able to convince herself that she was exactly as she had been this morning. Nothing had changed.

Yet everything had. This wasn't even her small oval mirror in the cabana. It was the huge, well-lit mirror in the Hers side of the master bathroom.

She hadn't argued with Everett about sharing his room. She felt awful for what he'd endured at her expense. He had barely got himself into the SUV to leave the hospital, moving as though he had been hit by a car. Plus, she hadn't wanted to stand there arguing with him, half-dressed, when she could come up here and take a few minutes to collect herself.

If only she didn't have to face him alone.

When they'd first returned to the mansion, there had been a chaos of people here. Some had been cleaning, others had been guards ensuring the mansion was secure, holding off reporters trying to take photos from the road and the water.

Freja had been anxiously waiting for them. The Italian couple clearly cared about Everett, but he had some kind of wall of resentment erected against them. Bianca had thought he was just being grumpy when he gave Giovanni one-word replies in the car, but Freja had briefly hugged him and when she had searched his expression, he had avoided her gaze and extricated himself, claiming he needed to sit down.

The couple had exchanged a resigned look that could have equally applied to one of their toddlers having a tantrum. It had been intriguing enough that when Freja asked Bianca if she would help her in the pool with the children, Bianca had agreed, hoping to learn more.

She had realized very quickly that she was being managed. Freja was providing the men a chance to speak privately, and it had gone against Bianca's best instincts to let Everett make any more decisions about her future without her input, but honestly? Cooling off in the pool with a pair of exuberant girls who were generous with affection had been an enormous stress reliever. When had she last laughed so unreservedly? Or chattered about daily life with another woman? Before her mother had died, she suspected. It had been nice. Normal.

Plus, Freja was so lovely, Bianca couldn't resent her machinations, especially when she asked her to reveal exactly what had happened to Everett, then grew choked up hearing it.

"He purposely put himself in hospital a year ago, so he could get a message to my foster mother. I didn't know he nearly *died*."

Bianca had wanted to hear more about that, but the children had distracted them.

Now the family was gone, along with the cleaners. The housekeeper was rearranging the kitchen back to the way she liked it and the guards had shooed off the worst of the photographers.

Bianca was cowering in this bathroom like a virgin on her wedding night.

She sighed, accepting that she couldn't hide forever. Not from the outside world and not from Everett.

With a twanging sense of exposure, she acknowledged how much she had already revealed about herself. Maybe she had kept the whistle-blowing from him that night they'd made love, but she had talked candidly about her life, telling him about her mother and her school years. Then she had completely given herself over to him.

At the time, she'd felt safe doing it, maybe because she had never expected to see him again, but now it felt like something he could use against her, leaving a shivering knot of apprehension sitting low in her belly.

She sighed, wishing they could go back to when he had held her in the garage. In that moment, she had started to think coming forward might be okay, if she had him on her side. She had started to trust him.

Oh, who was she kidding? She had thought him as handsome as ever, even with the stubble and black eye. Maybe because of it. His arms around her and his hard frame, so solid against her own, had felt exactly as good as the first time—reassuring and strong and tantalizingly hot. She had desperately wanted to know if he could still make her blood sizzle and her body soar the way he had six months ago. The only thing in her head had been, *Please kiss me again.*

He had. And it had been everything she remembered.

For a few seconds.

Now he probably wanted to throw her out on her ear.

There was only one way to find out. She pulled on a well-worn, halter-style sundress and combed out her hair, then went back outside to the patio.

For a second she thought he was dozing, but he turned his head and, *bam*, his blue gaze hit her like a tropical surf, crashing over her and filtering a soft tingle down her skin as his gaze went from her bared shoulders to her bare feet in cheap flip-flops.

She touched her damp hair, brushing a wet strand off her cheek that the breeze had picked up. She wished she had tied her hair back to hide the fading color. She wished she possessed makeup so she could have applied a small shield. The way she looked only emphasized that she had been living off his good graces all this time. She had very few assets and resources while he had a seemingly infinite amount, judging by the meal that had appeared like magic on the patio table.

"Are you hungry?" He swung his legs off the lounger and rose with a small wince.

"I am, actually." She pulled out her own chair, stomach pinching at the aroma off the paella still sizzling in its pan on the trivet. "No, thanks," she said of the wine he reached for. Best to keep her wits.

He left the bottle in the ice bucket and they both sat. His breath left him in a small grunt and her conscience was tugged yet again.

"I'm sorry. Truly." She waved him off from serving her and picked up his plate to serve him. "I'm sorry you were assaulted because of me. And the allergy, obviously. I didn't know about it, but now that I do, I'll be so careful in future." Did that sound as if she expected a future with him? The filled plate wobbled as she set it in front of him. "And the fake marriage," she added with a grimace, filling her own plate. "In my defense, I was trying to save your life, but I realize that I've made things awkward for you."

"You could add an apology for that colossal understatement," he said dryly. "It's the opposite of what I wanted to happen. All of those things are."

"I know. It's perplexing." She wrinkled her nose. "I've never been one of those people who is a walking disaster, but apparently that's my brand where you're concerned. Hashtag rom-coms are real."

"Are you seriously trying to make me laugh? My organs feel like they're dangling by threads inside my body."

"Sorry," she said, biting her lips. She scooped a morsel of chicken and rice and blew across it. "It's just I'm sure you're hating my guts by now and…" She didn't want him to hate her. The thought made her lonelier than she'd been all this time without anyone. Which made it even harder to say, "I would, um…" Her voice faltered. "I would completely understand if you wanted me to, um, do what you wanted me to do in the first place and say we don't know each other, then get lost." He wouldn't help her the way he'd offered. That was a given.

"It's too late for that," he dismissed tersely.

She had suspected it was an empty offer, but she had had to put it out there and there was no relief in his dismissing it. He was looking at her with that incisive gaze, making her own internal organs feel jiggly and hot-cold.

"What do you want me to do, then?"

"Help me sell this image of being happy honeymooners."

"Really? How?"

"We'll start with upgrading your wardrobe and fixing your hair. Then we'll make some appearances—"

"I meant how can we pretend to be happily married when we don't even know each other? But back up." A clang of alarm began ringing in her ears, making her voice quaver. "I realize a man like you can't have a wife who looks like a stranded castaway, but I can't afford a pile of new clothes." She had a small nest egg she was saving for legal fees and a little cash to bolt with. "The wardrobe I had in New York has probably been burned in effigy by now." If not by Troy, then by the flight attendant from whom she sublet.

"I'll take care of it," he dismissed, as though her interruption was inconsequential.

"That's very kind, Everett," she said through her teeth. "But I let a man give me expensive gifts and polish me up once before. Things didn't work out as well as I'd hoped. Don't tell me to do as I'm told," she held up a finger and waggled it. "You got your one free pass with that one."

His eyelids drooped with boredom. "Do we really need a long discussion on why you're uncomfortable with this arrangement only to arrive back at this point? You asked me what I want you to do. I'm telling you."

Her inner shaking increased, spreading into her hands as a burning tremble.

"So none of this is up for debate? Tell me, does the patriarchy issue union cards?" She tilted her head in facetious curiosity. "Can I see yours? Does it ever expire?"

"We're taking the long route through unnecessary argument, then?" He huffed a small noise of tested patience. "I am extremely wealthy, Bianca. I can afford to trick you out with the latest fashions. My image expects that you wear them, and your situation demands it. Think of it as armor. Troy Ackerley will exploit any sort of weakness you present. David and Goliath is a very heartwarming story, but Ackerley believes that might makes right. You need to match his wealth and power. Exceed it. Otherwise, he'll turn you into roadkill."

"Nice."

"Truth."

"And what do you get out of this? What do I owe you in exchange for a new wardrobe?"

Her abdomen tightened as she anticipated a demand for sex.

"Nothing." His cheek ticked. "Play your part well so this looks like a love match."

Was that pang inside her disappointment? Good grief, she was far too desperate for company if that was the case. Maybe she had lost all chances with him, given today, but did she even *want* a chance with him?

"Where does your wealth come from?" she asked.

His face blanked with surprise. "Family, mostly. Both of my grandfathers were successful industrialists. One was married to a princess, the other to the daughter of a real estate baron. My father patented some automotive technology that still pays out to me. Aside from squandering some of my fortune on cars—" he tilted his head toward the garage "—I invest wisely and live off the dividends."

"You've never held a real job?"

She saw a brief flash in his eyes before he dropped his gaze to his plate. "Like a paper route?" he drawled. "No." He chased it with a bite.

"No, Everett." She clapped her fork onto the table, sensing misdirection. "If you want me to trust you and go along with all of this, you have to be honest with me. I won't associate with someone who makes his money through immoral means." Couldn't and wouldn't. Her mother had set that example and she followed it. "That's why I had to expose Morris and Ackerley."

His gaze came up and she saw another flash, one that was his dominant personality surging to the fore, wanting to quash her for her outburst. But he pressed his mouth flat and ran his tongue over his teeth behind his lips. She watched a flicker in his expression as his mind seemed to weigh scales of pro and con.

"I did have a real job. For a decade and a half, working for the government. You'll have to accept that I can't tell you much, but that's why I can't have reporters digging around in my private life. This entire situation is *extremely* awkward," he pronounced facetiously.

She sat back, taking that in. "Can you tell me which part of government?"

"The part that gathers intelligence."

She lurched forward to hiss, "You were a spy?"

"Don't get excited." The corner of his mouth curled. "It was a lot of boring travel and a lot of boring paperwork. I could care less whether my martini is shaken or stirred."

"No," she dismissed, instinctually knowing that. "If it was boring, you wouldn't have done it. There must have been risk. Money. Power?"

He gave a small snort, as if he'd been caught before he'd found his hiding place.

"There was a certain amount of all those things," he downplayed. "And there was a competitive aspect. You have to think of information as a resource like any other. The first to discover it gets to exploit it."

"And sell it?"

"That happens," he allowed. "I was paid well enough I didn't need to extort anyone."

"Why did you quit? Not because of me?" She pressed a hand to where her belly began to churn.

"No, I quit before we met." He blinked and any sense of openness in his expression was gone. In fact, it darkened with displeasure. "Your situation became a gateway drug back into that work. Much as I didn't want to be connected, I thought it best to know exactly what I was mixed up in. I've spent the last six months gathering intel on Morris and Ackerley, following the money. When we sit down with your lawyers, I'll hand over the package. It should bolster the case against them. Maybe some funds will be recovered."

She opened her mouth to thank him but could see he didn't want her gratitude.

"You're anxious to put that work behind you? Why? Because it was dangerous?"

"Sometimes." He shrugged that off.

"Did Giovanni work with you?" she asked with sudden insight.

"See, these are the sorts of questions I don't want to be asked." His voice grew terse. "That's why you have to be my adoring wife for whom I would do anything, so people will believe that's the only reason I'm involved in your little tempest."

His sarcasm stung, telling her he disparaged such devotion, but she longed to be someone's adoring wife. She yearned for someone to be willing to do anything for her, even more so now she'd seen that Freja and Giovanni had exactly that.

She looked down at the fragrant, saffron-infused dish and didn't think she could take another bite.

The few options she still had left—going to her father or going on the run—were even less appealing than what Everett was offering. At least Everett would provide her the physical protection she needed along with legal help that could end the investigation more quickly.

And she owed him what protection she could provide in return. The way he'd brought her into this house was sketchy, but she was grateful for the security she had enjoyed these last months. She hadn't been scraping by, constantly looking over her shoulder.

On the contrary, she had been very comfortable aside from a thirst to see him again.

She blinked in a small wince at that piercing truth. She had wanted another chance to be close to him, to *really* get to know him. She still did, but she had to wonder if that was even possible. When she glanced up, he was looking at her with aggravation.

She was an encumbrance, dependent on him the way she had been on her mother, but at least her mother had loved her.

The fact Everett resented her could make their time together excruciating.

"How long would we have to pretend to be married?" she asked, voice rasping with vulnerability.

"A few weeks. Once things calm down, we can issue a statement that the media attention put too much pressure on our marriage and we're taking a break. Fade to a divorce announcement during a busy news cycle."

Her fake marriage was already dissolving? Bianca's brain tripped over her heart, trying not to hit the rough gravel of how quickly he was planning to dump her.

"And what—" She cleared her throat. "What are the rules?"

"Rules?" His brows went up.

"I realize you don't want sex, but if we're sharing a room—"

"I never said I don't want sex. I said I didn't *expect* it."

Her pulse swerved while he regarded her with that inscrutable look on his face.

Did she want to sleep with him again? Yes. But no. She wanted to sleep with the man she'd met six months ago, the one who wasn't so enigmatic and remote and shadowed by a secret past. She wanted to be the woman she used to be, the one with a life and a career, friends and a home. One who knew who she was. Not a stray. An orphan. A pariah in some circles. A ghost of the woman she'd been.

She wanted him to make her feel as though she excited and fascinated him. As though she was real and important, and he *liked* her.

Maybe some of her conflict showed on her face because he said abruptly, "Let's keep it simple. What are those rules for prom? No touching above the ribs or below the hips?"

"Perfect," she lied as her heart fell like a stone. She forced a smile and ate a bite of paella that coated her mouth like chalk.

"Now you tell me something. Why did you stay in Miami?" His voice was casual, but there was such an underlying lethality, her breath stalled in her lungs.

"I—You gave me a job and a place to stay." She found a shrimp and shoved it in her mouth.

"Oh, no, Bianca." His tone was gentle, but that

note of danger remained. "Look me in the eye and tell me why you wanted to stay in Miami."

The poor little shrimp sat in her throat as a sharp lump.

She lifted her lashes. They were heavy as cast iron. Meeting his gaze sent her stomach roiling. Her fingers tightened on her fork.

If she hadn't trained her whole life to compartmentalize this topic, she wouldn't have been able to prevaricate so blatantly. She had a brief thought that maybe he deserved to know, but this particular secret had been locked so far in her personal vault, it could never rise to bite him. He didn't need to know the whole truth, only the part he was asking about.

"This city feels like a connection to family. My mother grew up here and..." She forced the shrimp down with a sip of water. It lodged behind her heart. "As far as I know, my father still lives here." True enough. She hadn't looked him up lately. "Not that he knows I exist. Mom left him without telling him she was pregnant. She never liked to talk about him." She had, though. And when she did, she had impressed on Bianca that it was *their* secret, never to be repeated. "I can't tell you his name but believing in the possibility that I could meet him makes me feel... less untethered."

His brows went up. "I could find him for you."

A sting of alarm shot through her arteries. She

didn't doubt Everett could find anyone, given his bizarre skill set. She would love to think he was motivated by a desire to help her, but she had a feeling it was more about the challenge.

"What would I do?" she asked with a pained smile. "Turn up on his doorstep? Interrupt whatever life he's made with a new family?" That was a genuine reason she had never reached out to him. That and the fact her father was a Mafia kingpin whose life and family were in constant peril.

Even so, curiosity chewed at her deepest id. Her mother hadn't wanted to be associated with ill-gotten wealth, but Bianca constantly wondered what moral compromises were worth accepting if it meant she could finally meet her long-lost father.

What if he wanted nothing to do with her, though? She would be jeopardizing her own anonymity for nothing.

"Why the ruse about your grandmother?" Everett asked.

"Pardon?" She was jolted back by his question.

"I know your inheritance was real, but when we met, you made it sound like it had just happened. Why?" The quiet command in his tone told her he was determined to get every last grain of truth from her.

"Oh…um…what I told you on the plane

was mostly true. Mom was estranged from her mother and when I called to tell her that Mom had passed, she hung up on me." Bianca didn't mean for her voice to quaver when she said that, but it did. She stole a moment to push that particularly agonizing genie back into its bottle.

"I'm sorry, Bianca. That's cruel." His expression softened slightly, making the backs of her eyes grow hot.

"Someone told me once that people have all sorts of reasons to keep to themselves." She gave him a wobbly smile.

"Someone exceptionally wise, I imagine." His lips twisted in self-deprecating humor.

She dropped her gaze, not wanting him to see that she knew the elderly woman had most definitely had good reason to cut her daughter out of her life.

"About a year after Mom passed, I got the notice that my grandmother had left me her apartment. Troy and I were involved by then, but I didn't tell him." She had feared there would be questions about her father. "It sounds weird, but even though I didn't know yet that his business was dodgy, I didn't want him to pressure me into investing with Morris and Ackerley. Mom had always preached to me about how important it was for a woman to make her own financial decisions. To never let myself wind up in a position of being dependent."

Like now. She waited for him to say it, but he only watched her.

She took a slow, burning breath. "When Troy went away on business, I nipped down here, liquidated all my grandmother's assets and used most of it to pay off the last of Mom's medical bills. When I was getting ready to bolt, the apartment story made a good excuse to leave town. I doctored the original letter, mailed it to myself and acted super surprised. Troy was excited that I wanted to sell the apartment and use the money for our wedding and honeymoon. He couldn't put me on a plane fast enough."

His cheeks hollowed. "You're very sly beneath that sultry, damsel in distress persona, aren't you?"

She pretended that didn't sting, but it did. Deeply. Especially because she had to wonder if that wasn't her father's cold blood showing through in her veins.

"Not unlike a playboy who seduces a woman, then maneuvers her into living in his house. But married couples need something in common. Slyness can be ours." She smiled with false brightness.

"Along with not trusting one another." Cynicism coated his smile. "How fun."

CHAPTER FIVE

THEY NEEDED WEDDING photos to support their story.

Everett knew that doctored images would be disproven quicker than it would take to mock them up, so he called his former PA. She sent over a stylist for Bianca, a selection of gowns and a discreet photographer, who didn't hesitate to set his camera with an alternate time stamp. Everett tasked his housekeeper with sourcing a cake and spent an hour perusing jewelry, choosing a ten-carat Asscher Cut diamond in a platinum setting. The matching wedding band was coated in pavé diamonds. He also bought a matching necklace and earrings, sending those up to Bianca after the jeweler left.

He didn't know why people made such a fuss about organizing a wedding. He had everything arranged by the time he'd finished his lunch. All that was left was the honeymoon, according to the online checklist he consulted.

If only.

I realize you don't want sex...

For a moment, he had feared he was over-playing his hand, letting her know he was up for sex. Then he'd seen the hesitancy in her expression. As much as this attraction might still be burning brightly between them, she was too dependent on him for a no-strings affair, and her longing for family reinforced that he shouldn't lead her on.

Unfortunately, the more time he spent with her, the more he wanted her in every possible way. He wanted the secrets she wasn't telling him and her sarcastic little asides. He wanted to *touch* her. He wanted *her.*

Don't, he ordered himself, but his eyes were closing, and he was picturing her as she'd been that night they'd spent together, skin glowing with perspiration from their energetic lovemaking, lips swollen, eyes glazed with lust. He was thinking of her heat, her taste, her moans and the way her hips had danced as she straddled his hips.

A knock on his bedroom door brought him to an awareness that he'd been standing here brooding over her, proving how thoroughly she derailed his usually excellent concentration. Disgusted with himself, he finished pulling on his tuxedo and let in the stylist, who efficiently applied makeup to hide his black eye.

A short while later, he went outside where

Freja and Giovanni waited. A wedding needed guests, and Giovanni would have been Everett's best man if Everett had ever legally succumbed to marriage, so Everett had invited them. Giovanni wore a tuxedo, Freja was in a lovely off-the-shoulder gown in pale blue and the twins had matching dresses covered in frills.

Did Giovanni work with you?

Damn Bianca was smart. And good at lying. She had shamelessly suckered her fiancé on more than one occasion and threw out falsehoods like, *Yes, I'm his wife*, without hesitation. She hadn't been completely honest with him about her reason for staying in Miami, either. His well-trained ears had been crackling, trying to decipher the nuance in her voice, certain there was more to catch beneath the faltering way she had relayed how alone she was in the world.

That had got to him, despite his best defenses. He had seen the melancholy in her.

Didn't she realize that human connections were nothing but anguish? His mother was alive and healthy and lived a quiet life, but Everett's father had put her through hell. He'd put Everett through hell, first as a child who had worried about him alongside his mother, and later as an adult, when he had realized he resembled the man too closely.

Even Giovanni, who knew Everett better

than anyone, had put him in an impossible position that had forced him to make some terrible choices with painful consequences. He still carried a heavy weight on his conscience over that.

No. From the first time he had *looked* at Bianca, he had known he shouldn't approach her, that she would get under his skin, yet here he was, more worried about her than about what she could be doing to him. He was pretending to marry her, for God's sake. Not just forging some paperwork but putting on a romantic pageant to bolster the image.

He looked around at the way the setting sun filled the courtyard with golden light. Candles floated on the pool's still surface. Fairy lights adorned the umbrella that sat over a cake decorated with seashells and sea stars.

And they all waited for a bride, just like at a real wedding.

He opened his mouth to point out what a farce it was, but Bianca stepped from the house. He caught his breath.

She was all the more impactful for her subtlety. The strapless silk of her gown hugged her breasts and waist, then poured over her hips in frothy ivory, pooling around her feet.

Her bare shoulders gleamed like dark honey, setting off the diamond necklace around her throat. The earrings winked as they swung from her earlobes. Most of her hair was pulled up and interwoven with a string of pearls, but ringlets of tarnished bronze framed her face.

Bianca paused to take in the candles and atmosphere, and Louisa said in a breathy voice, *"Zia è molto carina, Mamma."*

"She is very pretty, isn't she?" Freja smoothed her daughter's hair.

Bianca ducked her head shyly, then accepted a bouquet of orchids from the housekeeper. The photographer stepped onto a chair and asked them to stand so the pool would form a backdrop.

Bianca picked up her gown as she walked toward Everett. Her steps slowed as her gaze met his. Maybe it was his imagination or maybe time itself stretched out. A soft breeze played with the fine strands of hair against her cheek and her breasts lifted against the confines of her dress as she drew in a breath.

It's fake, Everett kept reminding himself, but music was playing in his head as she approached. Not the pedestrian wedding march, but something from the night they had met—a lazily paced, sexy, moody song. Violin strings sauntered as Etta James's powerful, emotive voice crooned "At Last"…

He tried to ignore it. Tried to look away from this vision approaching him, but the damp sheen on her eyes shot out like an arrow to pierce his breastbone.

"What's wrong?" He instinctively reached for her hand, hearing that his voice was far too thick for his liking.

Her self-deprecating smile fell away, and her expression flinched.

"This wedding isn't even real, but I can't help wishing my mother was here." The candles reflected in the poignant sadness that filled her eyes. The corners of her mouth trembled.

Without conscious thought, he cupped the side of her neck and caressed beneath her ear. Damn, he'd been aching to touch her again. Kissing her had nearly killed him, but he was staring at her unsteady mouth and wanted to press his own against it with reassurance. He wanted to draw her in and protect her from sad ghosts and wistful wishes.

"That's really good," the photographer murmured. "Step closer and put your hand on his chest. Look smitten."

A small flinch crossed her expression. It bothered him, too. She might withhold some things, but her heartache was real. It shouldn't be misused for a lie they would feed to the press, but as she shifted closer, her pulse grew rapid against his palm. Her lashes lifted and conflict swirled behind her eyes—yearning and defensiveness, desire and memory.

So many hot, delicious memories.

"Pretend you're about to kiss?" the photographer prompted.

Everett slid his arm behind her back. She was pliant, allowing him to draw her closer. In fact, she leaned into him in that delicious melting way that short-circuited his brain. His hand found her tailbone. Her body heat radiated through slippery silk to brand his palm. His heart began to thud even harder.

Her fingers came up to play with his ear, sending the most exquisite shivers across his skin. A groom ought to desire his bride, but that's not what either of them was. He shouldn't be twitching and swelling, reflexively dragging her closer so her breasts flattened tantalizingly against his chest. He shouldn't be fantasizing about carrying her over the threshold of his bedroom and placing her on his bed.

Her breath shortened and she tilted her chin to offer her mouth.

Pretend. He bent his head but made himself stop short and held the position as the camera clicked and his whole body turned to concrete with tension. They were already breaking the rules they'd set. His hand was splayed on the top of her bottom. His other was against her rib cage, the heel of his palm resting against the side swell of her breast, fingertips tickling at the edge of her gown where the warm skin under her arm beckoned.

When her light touch found the hollow at the base of his skull, and twitched in subtle invitation, he broke and crashed his mouth onto hers.

This was the kiss he had wanted this morning. Electrifying heat shot through him, and she arched as though she'd been struck by lightning. Plush lips clung to his. The damp tip of her tongue grazed the inside of his lip, and he stole a deeper taste of her. She quivered and pressed harder into him. He hauled her closer, consuming her.

They had an audience, two of them children, but he didn't care. Maybe the photographer even said, "That's good," in a way that suggested the kiss could end.

Never. Everett ignored everything except the sensation of Bianca's hands roaming across his back. He greedily ravished her, filling his hands with her, thinking only one thing. *At last.*

"Theresa, no!"

If they had all stayed exactly as they were, nothing would have happened. The toddler would have run up, grabbed Bianca's dropped bouquet and handed it back to her. That's all the little girl was trying to do.

But the photographer was coming off his chair and instinctively tried to protect his precious equipment. He stumbled and caught himself on the table. The scraping sound of the table legs triggered Everett's most sharply honed reflexes. He jerked up his head and, while his one arm tightened around Bianca, securing her against him, he pressed out a hand to guide the toddler away from the edge of the pool.

Even that would have been fine. He would have stepped back and caught his balance, and it would have all been completely fine.

But Bianca was also startled. *She* tried to place herself between the little girl and the pool edge. She collided into Everett. Their feet tangled. The lip of the pool edge provided exactly the right slope for her sharp heel. She slipped and lost her footing.

That was it. Her weight landed against him. His injured knee buckled and they were falling. There was nothing Everett could do except catch his breath before they hit the water in a mighty splash.

The photo was tracking really well, Bianca noted as she checked her new smartphone.

It had been two days since the doomed photo shoot, four since Everett had shown up so unexpectedly. In that time, he had provided her with all the latest gadgets along with so many clothes she spent half the day in fittings. The rest of the time, she sat in meetings with lawyers and PR specialists. She rarely had a moment alone, especially with him.

So she didn't know what he thought of the

photo. Probably that it was insult to injury after a previous injury and one before that, she thought dourly. But after viewing the staged almost-kiss that the photographer had managed to take before they fell, they decided this one looked the most authentic with its candid lack of elegance. Most of the candles had been gutted by their splash. Their clothes were soaked through and ruined, but with the underwater lights glowing behind them, she and Everett were silhouetted in waist-high water, the backlighting hiding his injuries really well.

It also showed him reaching for her. He'd been doing it as much to steady himself on his one leg as to ensure she was upright and breathing. He'd been furious, growling, "First rule of this marriage is no more attempts to kill me."

It had been wrong to laugh, but she had. In the photo, her head was thrown back, her profile one of unrestrained delight. Her exposed throat was vulnerable and trusting. Everett was grasping her possessively, head tilted in a way that dominated, but also suggested protectiveness. Tender, almost.

He'd been *so* annoyed, which shouldn't have made it funnier, but it had. Thankfully, none of his impatience came through in the image. He was starkly beautiful, seemingly mesmerized by her.

Judging by the comments, everyone thought they were deeply in love.

Bianca nearly believed it herself when she looked at the photo. Or rather, she wanted to believe she could experience love like that, love that was unforeseen and grand and joyful. A love that loved her back even when she was messy and clumsy and ruinous. Love that was willing to save her when she was in trouble.

She knew that sort of love was a figment created by Hollywood to sell popcorn. Dating had been enjoyable when she had made time for it, but she had never been so moved by anyone that she couldn't take or leave that particular person. Troy had been her most intense relationship, and she had always felt a little manipulated by his over-the-top romantic gestures, as though he was using them as leverage to guilt her into whatever he wanted from her. It hadn't felt like what she wanted love to be.

Of course, she had always heeded her mother's advice to keep her heart well guarded. Her mother had loved her father her whole life. Her heartbreak had always been obvious when she talked about the difficult decision she'd made in leaving him. *I was immersed in his life, and it was a life I didn't want. One I feared I wouldn't survive.*

That was the real reason Bianca had been compelled to expose Troy's crimes. She had started to repeat her mother's history, attaching herself to a man who broke laws for his own gain. She hadn't even loved Troy, not the way her mother had loved her father. Her mother had already been gone, but the guilty knowledge that Bianca was letting her down had far outweighed any affection or loyalty she'd felt toward Troy.

She had thought that tepid mix of gratitude and companionship was all she was capable of feeling toward a man.

Until she met Everett.

She couldn't say why their connection had felt so profound and real from the very beginning. It *wasn't* real, she scolded herself. It was a trick of lust and isolation. She had played a hoax on herself by reliving their night again and again, allowing herself to believe his feelings ran deeper than they did.

Whatever he had felt that night hadn't been mentioned again. Sure, he'd kissed her before their dunk in the pool, but he avoided her during the day, came to bed after she was asleep and rose before she woke.

His indifference reinforced the impression that he would rather leave her on the bottom of a pool than pull her out of one.

She tried not to let his lack of interest bother her, but it did. She felt as though she had disappointed him, or he begrudged her. If he hadn't been providing the protection and advisors she needed, she might have struck out on her own.

Her mother had never prepared her for this, she thought ironically. Rather than becoming dependent because she'd fallen in love, it was the opposite. She had no choice but to rely on him, and he didn't seem to give two hoots about her.

"Is that the Montrachet Grand Cru?"

Everett's voice startled her into dropping her phone into her lap. She usually spent this hour before dinner curled up on the sofa with only her phone and glass of wine for company.

"I wanted to try it before I order a few cases." He poured one for himself.

"Order me one," she joked. "I really like it." She picked up her glass and drank in the aromas of earth and pear, then let the cool lick of smoky butterscotch pour across her tongue. There was a tang of orange peel before it finished with smooth vanilla.

"It's five thousand dollars a bottle."

She nearly spit her wine back into her glass. Instead, she took a big gulp to catch the ice cube she'd dropped into it because she had let it grow warm.

As he came to sit across from her, nerves closed in on her. She had been wanting one-on-one time with him, thinking it would clear the air in some way, but the air became charged and weighted.

Fortunately, her phone pinged, allowing her to duck her head to read the message as she swallowed the half-melted ice cube.

"Freja," she said as she set her phone aside. "She's been checking in with me a lot. I guess she has some experience with being reluctantly famous."

Freja's father had been a renowned travelogue writer. Freja's memoire-turned-movie had made her a celebrity in her own right, not to mention the surprising fact her husband had been pronounced dead for a time.

Bianca was dying to ask Everett about that. She had read what she could find online, but a lot of links were broken—which struck her as suspicious, but the one photo she'd found of the press conference when Giovanni reappeared showed Everett by his side.

"Freja asked me if we were going to her premiere," Bianca continued, chattering nervously. "I said I didn't think it would be a good idea. I'm too notorious and would steal her thunder. She said this is actually the fifth opening after viewings at film festivals and a big thing in Hollywood. She said that, if anything, the film would benefit from the buzz we would cause, but she didn't mean that as pressure for us to turn up."

"I've been thinking about it." Everett was

swirling his glass and poked his nose into the bowl before sipping. The face he made couldn't have been in reaction to the wine. It was excellent. "Given all the celebrities, the security will be very tight. It's an ideal place to debut as a couple. Showing up is the least I can do for Freja."

He cared about that family; she knew he did. She had caught him smirking affectionately at the little ones, even though he kept his distance.

"I asked Freja about the work you used to do," she admitted. "She said she couldn't talk about it, but that she understands how curious and frustrated I must feel. I guess that means Giovanni did work with you."

She didn't make it a question and she wasn't surprised by the hard stare of warning he sent her.

"Can you tell me how you met him, at least? Or is that classified, too?"

"No. It's just painful." His expression turned stoic. "His brother, Stefano, was a close friend at boarding school. I met him when some older boys thought it would be a funny prank to sneak crushed peanuts into my soup. I would have died if Stefano hadn't got me help."

"That's horrible! But how did Giovanni not know of your allergy until last year?"

"Because I became very careful about who I told," he said in a hard voice. "I thought that was the best approach, managing it myself, discreetly, until you exploited that weakness the other day."

He didn't give her a chance to defend herself, continuing on.

"Giovanni was younger, not there when it happened. Their father was a diplomat, and they moved a lot, but I stayed in touch with Stefano until he died in the same car crash that killed their parents. That's how Giovanni lost his legs. He was alone in hospital for months after. I visited him as often as I could."

"Oh." She clapped a hand over her breaking heart. "He must have been so lonely. That's really nice that you were there for him."

"I wasn't being nice. I was grieving, too. Not just Stephano, who was my only real friend, but my father." He looked into his wine. "After his brain injury, I lost the man I knew. Half the time Giovanni and I played video games without speaking more than ten words, but it got us through a difficult period."

"Yet you're borderline hostile toward him now. What changed? Do you resent that Freja came between you?"

"I know she calls me his ex," he said pithily.

Bianca hadn't heard that and bit her lips to hide her amusement.

"My feelings toward him are not, and never have been, romantic. Even if they were, how could I resent her? She's his perfect complement and he deserves to be happy." He drank deeply, expression faraway and contemplative.

"Do you envy him that happiness?"

"No." That came out prompt and firm. His cool gaze snapped to hers, seeming to carve his next words indelibly into her soul. "The higher you soar, the farther you fall. I saw how wrecked he was by loss. More than once." His gaze shifted to the darkening sky beyond the windows. "I wouldn't subject myself to that. Ever."

"*That* sounds lonely," she said with a catch behind her heart. "I ache for a family. I feel empty not having anyone." That's why she had yearned for her grandmother to embrace her after her mother had passed. That's why she was tempted every single day to reach out to her father and half siblings.

"You can have one," Everett said, making her heart swerve. "When this is over."

With someone else. That's what he was really saying with that dispassionate look.

She swallowed the lump that rose in her

throat. It stuck itself, jagged and hard, behind her sternum.

"But pretend that's what you and I are embarking on now?" she asked with a creak in her voice.

"Yes."

It was exactly as she had known things were, but hearing it, absorbing it, made the ache in her chest all the harder to bear.

CHAPTER SIX

THEY ATTENDED THE PREMIERE. Everett's conscience wouldn't let him snub his friends again. *You're borderline hostile toward him.*

Everett hadn't meant to come across that way. He had been giving them space to push him out of their lives as he deserved. He chafed at the way Bianca kept pulling them back into his sphere so he had to constantly confront his guilt.

As if he didn't wear self-loathing as a cape all day, every day.

It had a new lining, though. One that was slippery as satin, hot and cold in turns. Bianca.

He'd been trying to ignore her since the poolside kiss. Thank God they'd fallen in, or they may never have stopped. He'd been avoiding her as much as possible, trying to dodge further temptation, leaving her in meetings with interview coaches and spending his own time ensuring the circle of security around them was impenetrable.

He couldn't ignore her tonight, though. He could barely take his eyes off her.

His tux had been replaced after the photo debacle and Bianca was in a stunning, sequined gown. Her hair had been corrected to a rich brunette that fell around her face in screen star waves. Her makeup was subtle, allowing her natural beauty to shine brighter than the diamonds she wore.

"Is my makeup smudged?" she asked with a trace of dread as she glanced across the back seat of the SUV and caught him staring. Her hand came up.

"No." She was breathtakingly perfect. "I was thinking that you'll be asked who you're wearing."

"The stylist told me Versace."

"The jeweler is local." He told her the name.

"These are real?" she hissed, touching the necklace. "I thought all of this was costume. I've been leaving them lying around like old shoes."

"I noticed," he said dryly. "But the house is secure. We'll put them in the room safe tonight."

"Why are we staying at the hotel?" she asked with a distracted frown.

"Appearances."

"Hmph. Still, why don't I just give them back to the jeweler, so I don't have to worry about them?"

"Because I bought them."

"You did not." She glared at him.

He lifted a negligent shoulder. "Appearances." And he had thought they would suit her. They did. The warm tones in her complexion were emphasized by the platinum setting and her electrifying presence was amplified by the sparkle of the stones.

"Well, I don't accept that burden of worry," she informed him. "I have enough of those on my plate, thanks." She leaned to peer through the window as the limo slowed.

They had joined the queue approaching the red carpet out front of the theater. Her profile grew apprehensive.

Everett had been in his share of media scrums, but Bianca was new to this. When they emerged a few minutes later, the roar of the crowd rolled over them as a reverberating wave. Her fingernails dug through his sleeve, and he noted how she tried to use him as a shield against the flashing cameras.

A surge of protectiveness had him pulling her close. He brushed off the request that they pose and make remarks and drew her into the theater.

"Are you all right?" he asked as he found a quiet corner. For the most part, she was very self-possessed and confident. It hadn't occurred to him she would be so overwhelmed.

"I'm feeling a little like Cinderella, going from only having the birds as company to this."

Her stark gaze took in the melee of celebrities and VIP guests. Waiters with trays of champagne circulated and they each accepted one.

"Is Cinderella the polyamorous one who took up with seven small-statured miners?" Everett asked conversationally.

"Do brush up on your fairy tales, Everett. She's the indentured servant who dropped a shoe and turned into a pumpkin."

"The one who dropped her *luggage*." He nodded. "That tracks."

"Hilarious." But she suppressed a smile, and that pleased him since he'd been trying to put her at ease.

He was sorely tempted to kiss that smile. She would be a lot easier to resist if he wasn't constantly picturing her wet lashes and dripping hair and chilled nipples pressing against silk. If he wasn't hearing her laughter when she got a video of the children from Freja or wasn't forced to stand so close right now. The heat of her body was radiating against his while she wore a look of wonder.

"I have to say, you do know how to impress a girl. If I forget to tell you later, I had a good time tonight."

"You have a crystal ball in that little purse of yours?"

"Seriously?" Her cheeky smile faded. "It's a movie quote from that other well-known fairy tale, *Pretty Woman*. You must have seen it at least once. Julia Roberts?"

"Is that the one where she sues the company for poisoning the water?" He knew it wasn't.

"You're hopeless," she declared, but they were both hiding smirks of enjoyment.

Their flirting was interrupted as they were ushered to their seats. They watched an engaging movie that had him sincerely complimenting Freja when they saw her at the after-party in the hotel ballroom.

She and Giovanni were much in demand, so they only spoke to them for a moment. Then Everett kept hold of Bianca's hand as they circulated.

In maintaining his cover, he had attended thousands of parties like this so it was inevitable that he would bump into people who knew him as a globe-trotting playboy. A few even knew him from his other role in intelligence. They all wanted to congratulate him on his marriage and meet his notorious wife.

Everett introduced her but kept all the interactions very brief while behaving as solicitously as a newly married man ought to seem toward his bride. Did he take advantage of the excuse to touch her? He tried not to, but the way her voice faltered when his hand absently drifted to her lower back, and pink rose under her cheeks, made him realize he was having an effect on her.

At that point, it took all his discipline not to draw a line up her spine to explore the sensitive skin at her nape, to see if he could deepen her blush. His gaze wanted to travel to the swells of her breasts, to see if they were lifting in an uneven rhythm against the line of her gown.

It was a tipping point, one where he ought to have called a halt to the evening and saved them both. Instead, he let it go on and, a few minutes later, the music started. It was not the staid waltz of a charity gala. It was loud and lively, and Bianca glanced with longing to where the crowd began bumping and grinding to the beat.

"Do you want to dance?" He could see she did.

Eagerness lit up her expression. "Do you? I haven't gone dancing since college."

He couldn't deny her. No, that was a lie. He didn't want to deny himself. It was only dancing, he chided himself as he shrugged out of his jacket and hung it over the nearest chair. He waved an invitation for her to lead him into the flailing bodies.

She set down her drink and her arms were already climbing over her head as she entered the fray, hips swaying hypnotically.

Everett danced the way he did everything else—with competence and without drawing undue attention, but Bianca was genuinely good.

She had natural rhythm and the way she moved was sinuous and sexy as hell.

As she loosened up, she picked up her skirt at the top of the slit, exposing more of her thigh while she stepped and shimmied. Half a song later, she took hold of his shoulder and made a figure eight with her hips, dipping and climbing, then trailed her hand down his chest and around his waist as she circled him.

He felt the vibration of a groan in his throat, one drowned out by the pounding music. Whether she was playing a part or was simply lost in the moment, he couldn't tell. It didn't matter to the flesh behind his fly. He responded as though she was working him up for their mutual pleasure, and the more she lost herself to sensuality, the harder it was to remember why he didn't want to give in to this incessant tug of want.

She wanted things he didn't, he recalled. They might be sexually compatible, but their lives and aspirations weren't. She was dependent on him.

She came back around, and he watched her turn twice before he gave into temptation and closed in on her, pulling her back into his front. He pinned his hips to her rocking bottom, letting her feel his arousal so she knew exactly how he was reacting to her.

She didn't balk. Her hand climbed to curl behind his neck, and he pressed his jaw to her temple, following her every move. Her stomach was tense against his splayed hand. The backs of her thighs rubbed hotly against the fronts of his. Her hair got him drunk on the aroma of almonds and orange blossoms and her bottom ground into his erection.

He started to think maybe none of those other things mattered. Maybe, they could keep it physical.

Maybe he was dancing with danger and maybe he didn't care.

Before Bianca realized it, their lighthearted fun became foreplay. One moment laughter was bubbling in her chest, the next her pulse was thudding with the music, her skin sensitized to every sensation.

With each brush of their bodies and skim of his hands, desire unfurled a little more within her, overriding her inhibitions while her memory of their night teased her to, *Do it again. See if it's the same*.

The way Everett touched her was reminiscent of their lovemaking—as though he was worshipping her with his hands. As though their bodies were in such perfect accord, they moved as one. As though he wanted her more than he wanted anything else in life. She was the only thing that mattered.

It was so intoxicating, she turned to face

him and curled her arm around his neck, then touched the back of his head, urging him to bring his ear down to her mouth. He was tense and his expression forbidding, but the intriguing thickness pressing into her abdomen encouraged her.

"Do you want to go upstairs?"

His hands on her hips tightened deliciously before he lifted his head and looked at her from beneath hooded eyelids. His nod was barely perceptible, and his hands fell away.

A flush of nervous excitement engulfed her. She led him through the writhing bodies back to their table, suddenly feeling drunk even though she'd only had a couple glasses of champagne.

She glanced over her shoulder as they walked to the elevator. His expression was unreadable, but he carried his jacket in front of him, filling her with amused, heady power.

As they stepped inside the car, she pressed herself to the side wall, expecting him to crowd against her and kiss her passionately the way she was longing for him to do.

He used his key to activate the *P* button and leaned on the far wall, regarding her with a flinty look. Her buzz of arousal stumbled into uncertainty. A prickle of inadequacy began to cool the sultry heat that gripped her.

"Is something wrong?" She knew they'd agreed to different rules, but...

"I want to be sure you're not still caught up in fairy tales. Everything that has happened tonight has been part of our act. You know that, don't you?"

Her heart lurched.

"Everything?" The banter? The way he had held her hand and solicitously asked if she was all right? The way he had just danced with her as though they were already making love?

Her ego took that straight on the chin, but she lifted it the way any good boxer did when they still had some grit left in them.

"Your body should win an award for its performance then. Why bother hiding it if all of this is for show?"

He kept hold of her gaze. The air crackled as he absorbed her scathing remark.

"My erections are biology. They're not a promise or a sign of growing affection or an attempt to make that family you said you long for."

The elevator arrived at their floor with a gentle halt, but his words jolted with the force of an earthquake. As the doors opened, guards immediately requested their identification.

She stood there dumbly while Everett took care of it.

If she had had any choice, she might have walked right back into that elevator and out the front doors of the hotel, but all she wanted in this moment of mortification was to hide. She subtly kept Everett from touching her elbow and accompanied him down the hall. They passed guards stationed at all the doors of these top floor suites, so she didn't speak.

"We swept when we placed your luggage inside, sir," the one at their door said. "We can do it again now if you'd like."

"I'll do it." Everett used his key card to open their door and stepped inside to hold the door for her. Then he moved methodically around the room, running his hand beneath shelves and table edges, following sight lines to the sofa and into the bedroom and bathroom.

"Do you really think someone would bug our room?" she asked with equal parts disbelief and mockery.

"Allowing yourself to believe no one would is how you wind up compromised."

Hmph. She should probably be grateful for his vigilance. Being in the headlines was invasive enough. She didn't need nude photos undermining her credibility where Morris and Ackerley were concerned, but she was still affronted by his attitude in the elevator.

She sat to remove her shoes, throat aching with something worse than rejection. Humiliation. She only wished she could claim she'd been acting, but it was too late for that, not when she was the one who had suggested they come up here. She didn't even want to face him after being so blatant about her desire.

"Clear." He came back from the bedroom and headed straight to the bar, where he cracked a bottle of Scotch. "What were we talking about?"

"I don't remember," she said dourly.

"No?" He sent her a sideways look, one brow cocked. "That's fine." He set out two glasses and poured the drink into the first. "Will you have Scotch, or do you want something else?"

"I know the difference between fantasy and reality, Everett."

"Oh, *that's* what we were talking about. Let's make it a sober conversation, then." He set aside the bottle and came to the sitting area empty-handed. He took the armchair like a dissolute king, dropping into it and studying her as though she were some lowly petitioner.

Her skin tightened and her throat dried, but she managed to ask, "What's there to talk about? You were acting as though you wanted to have sex with me, but it was just an act. My mistake." She picked up the skirt of her gown so she could get her knees under her and resettled with a huff.

"Is that all you want? You're horny so you want sex?"

"Excuse me?" Her chest and cheeks were already scalded with ire. Now they burned hotter than the backs of her eyes.

"There's no shame in it. You're coming off a dry spell. That's also biology."

"Just because you pick up lovers like frequent-flyer points doesn't mean *I* don't know how to be alone." She rose, too offended to face him.

"It's been a spell for me, too," he said flatly. "One of the exact duration as yours."

She faltered, turning around with disbelief.

He cocked a brow.

She shook her head and looked out the window. Much as she wanted to believe his celibacy had something to do with her, she wasn't that delusional.

"Spending time together, pretending to be in love, was always going to put us at risk for this, Bianca. All I'm saying is, don't start believing we have anything more than we do."

"You have to know a person to fall for them. We're still practically strangers."

"Why do you want to have sex with me, then?" he asked gently. "Because you don't have sex with strangers. I knew that the first time we were together."

"When I had sex with a stranger?" she asked caustically, then sighed. "I like the way you make me feel, okay?" It wasn't quite true. Emotionally, she felt so much yearning it was rending her apart.

She drooped her forehead against the cool glass, hating herself for being so susceptible to him because when he touched her, she condensed like a supernova, becoming a ball of light and energy and glittering joy. The way he'd shaped her waist and hips as they danced had sent tendrils of need climbing upward from her belly. He had guided her in ways that made her think every move was her own, then he had perfectly matched each step, as though they were intrinsically connected. The flex of his muscles, the way he'd watched her as though she was the only person in the room, had made her *want*. Want to touch him, want to kiss him and strip for him and take him inside her.

No one else had ever made her feel like that, and it hurt, physically opened a cavernous ache inside her, to think she would never feel that way again.

"I've spent six months wondering if we're still as potent a combination as we were that night." The lust in his voice matched the sizzling embers sitting in the base of her throat and the bottom of her heart and the pit of her stomach. It made her breath catch.

Her shoulder blades tensed and tingled, and her gaze was pulled from the view to lock with his, but there was no smile there. No warm glow of affection in his burning gaze.

He wasn't any happier with this pull than she was.

"When you were pushing up against me on

the dance floor I wanted to take you into a stall of the men's room. I would have had you over the edge of a table if I could have."

Neither of them moved, but her whole body began to quiver. His blatant talk sent a spike of fresh arousal into her, one that made her feel loose and drugged. Dizzy with carnal hunger.

Truth was, it hadn't really gone away. It had only been veiled by petulance and denial on her part, thwarted by his ruthless self-discipline and annoyingly tough demand to be in control of everything, including her.

That realization made her heart lurch. He was far better at resisting his reaction to her than she was to him. He had been three steps ahead of her from the first time they spoke, and still was. She was hopelessly outmatched, which meant that any loss in this relationship would be borne by her.

"I will happily make all of your sexual fantasies come true, Bianca." His tone was both a licentious promise and a grim warning. "But that's all it will be. You have to know that and accept it before we do anything in that bed besides sleep."

She curled a fist, trying to find a semblance of self-protection. Trying not to betray that she was willing to accept any terms, so long as it meant he would touch her.

"Be careful what you offer." She leaned her

shoulder against the glass and glanced out, trying to find an idle tone. "You're talking to a woman who has spent six months reading romance novels. I have thousands."

"Of fantasies?" In his translucent reflection, he sat taller. His voice lowered an octave, so it was deeply intimate and darkly curious. "I've never read one. Tell me what happens."

Her knees weakened. She locked them and forced herself to say facetiously, "A lot of virgins are seduced by ruthless tycoons. Which one do you want to be?" She turned her head to bat her lashes at him.

His head went back, and his eyes narrowed with consideration. "My first time wasn't my best look. That's when I learned that success doesn't always mean arriving first."

She bit her lip, hating him a little when he was like this—human and endearing.

"I've never actually seduced a virgin and since I already have the costume, I'll be the tycoon." He loosened his tie. "What happens?"

"I was joking." She cleared her throat and sent a look of desperation out the window, but her body was reacting to everything. His confidence and command. The way his body radiated power and the way his expression had settled into watchfulness.

She was becoming his sole focus and it made her skin tighten. She had to cross her arms and hug them against breasts that began to swell and tingle. Her pulse was tripping and quickening.

"Tell me," he insisted softly. "I'm ruthless, remember? I'll get it out of you one way or another. Why am I ruthless, by the way?"

"You tell me," she said with false brightness. "It's also not a great look. You might want to work on that."

A slow smile stretched across his lips. "I like that you're already getting into it. Tell me about your first time. Is it worth reenacting?"

"*No.* It was me trying to find out why everyone thought sex was such a big deal. I never really got an answer to that."

"No?"

Her heart lurched. Until him. That's what she should have said.

"Let's fix that," he suggested in that compelling tone.

He was all the way across the room, and she was practically melting the glass with her body heat, thinking she would fall through it at any moment.

"Why am I deflowering you?" he asked.

"Stop." She ignored the nervous excitement slithering into her middle. "This is silly."

"It's a fantasy," he said quietly. "One that we can stop anytime. If you want to stop now, that's fine."

His words rocked her to the soles of her feet.

She set splayed fingertips on the window to steady herself, but maybe he was right. Maybe it was the best way to ensure she didn't take their lovemaking too seriously.

And maybe she was rationalizing so she didn't have to deny herself something she wanted with every cell in her body.

"You want to seduce me into giving up my virtue as revenge against my father. I'm trying to save his business, but you'll probably ruin him the way he ruined you. You're willing to use me to humiliate him."

"I want to send you back to him guilty that you slept with his enemy and *liked* it."

Oof. He caught on fast. She swallowed. "I don't care about myself, but my secret half sister will be left penniless if my father loses all his money. You don't know that part."

"Then why tell me?"

"Exactly. You're too contemptuous to care. All you think about is your quest for revenge. You'll be merciless in exacting it."

"I will."

He rose and adrenaline soared up through her arteries. A rush of fight or flight burned in her muscles as he came toward her.

His expression was so carnal and pitiless, she pressed her back to the window and held her breath. Her hand came up to his chest as he caged her by leaning his forearms on either side of her head. His lips were so close to hers, her mouth felt sparks of static jumping between them. Her breasts rose and fell unevenly, *almost* brushing his shirt.

"Your father consigned my best friend to a wheelchair. Mention his name and I will walk out and take my vengeance in other ways. Perhaps on your poor sister."

Her scrambled brain tried to catch up. "Did you just give me a safe word? Everett."

She covered her heart, weirdly moved beneath her lewd excitement. She'd never had a safe word, never imagined needing one. She hadn't imagined it would feel so profound. It forged an immediate bond of trust between them, which was silly. This was a *game*.

"Do you have one?" she asked.

"No," he said simply, and somehow, that didn't surprise her a bit.

He took hold of her chin. "But if you mention any other man's name when you're in my bed, I assure you I'll leave you panting in a state of heat." He scraped his thumb across her bottom lip. "Now quit trying to play on my sympathy. I have none. This is a transaction, and you'd better do exactly as I say or the deal is off."

He released her and rocked back on his heels.

She was pinned by a fearful thrill, heart pounding. "Really?"

"Find out. Get in that bedroom and wait for me." He jerked his chin toward the door.

"N-naked?" Her head swam.

"No. I like my toys in mint condition. I'll unwrap you myself." He didn't look at her as he moved to push a hand into the pocket of his discarded jacket. When he noticed her still leaning weakly against the window, he commanded, "*Go.*"

CHAPTER SEVEN

THE PUNCH OF thrill that sent her into the bedroom faded to nerves once she was there. Why was he making her wait for him? Left alone, her head began filling with tumbling second thoughts and hurry-up anticipation. Not knowing what he intended to do to her was excruciating.

She had been thinking about their first night for six months, yearning to repeat it. On that night, he had seduced her slowly with small gestures that she could have easily rebuffed if she hadn't been into it. A light caress on her wrist, a slip of her hair over her ear, a kiss on the boardwalk. She'd been more than a willing participant by then, moaning when he'd kissed her neck in the elevator. She had been weak with want.

Since then, she had longed to be swept away again. For possibility to become probability, then reality.

This was different. It was happening, yet it wasn't. She had no doubt she could back out, no hard feelings, but she wasn't so much afraid of what was about to happen as jittery at the uncertainty of not knowing. She had never role-played a fantasy. In that respect, she did feel like a virgin. Would she do it right? Would she like it? Would he?

He had grasped onto his part with such brutal ease, she was daunted. She knew the point was to commit to the role and play it out to its conclusion. She wanted that, but it meant giving up control to him. Letting him guide and take the lead and *have his way*.

Another shiver of dread-filled anticipation went through her, followed by a rush of incendiary heat.

The door clicked and he entered. His shoes were gone. His tie still hung loosely around his neck. He made a point of closing the door with a firm click, then stood with his arms folded, shoulders straining the fabric of his shirt, weight balanced evenly between his braced feet. He was a potent man intent on ravishing her and her knees nearly buckled in capitulation.

He sauntered toward her, pulling his loosened tie over his head as he closed in.

"Cross your wrists."

"Are you serious?" she gasped, tucking her fists beneath her neck.

"It's only to remind you who you belong to." He met her gaze as he took hold of her wrist, slowly drawing it down, watching closely and giving her plenty of time to refuse.

Her heart was crashing around in her chest, but he was watching to make sure she was with him, exactly as he had the first time. It was weirdly reassuring.

In a small daze, she let her other arm come down and crossed it over the first. He wound the loop of silk around her wrists and gave it a tug.

She wriggled slightly. It was snug, but she could pull herself free if she really wanted to. At the same time, the small constraint seemed to tug her deeper into the game they were playing. She threw her head back to glare at him.

"Now lie back and think of England?" she challenged.

"I will not have a sacrificial lamb in my bed." His smile was cruel. "Your pleasure will very much be my pleasure. Harder to meet your father's eyes that way." His fingertip traced her lips in a tickling caress that had her rolling them inward, unable to erase the sensation. "Which you would know if you weren't so inexperienced."

She was. In this moment, she was confronted by a man who far outclassed her in worldliness. In willpower. Whatever she thought she knew about men and sex and herself would be completely rewritten tonight. She knew that as a fact.

"Where is the zipper on this thing?" His arms came around her, drawing her into bumping against his front as he felt along her spine.

Her arms were trapped between them, and his erection brushed the back of her wrist. He slowly released her gown so it gaped across her breasts, nearly exposing them.

She gave a small gasp and reflexively tried to catch it.

"Shy? I haven't even started." His breath tickled a few loose strands of hair against her ear.

A shiver trailed down her nape. She tried not to sway, but the press of his palm against her bared spine tilted her into him. His other hand brushed her hair back from her cheek and his mouth went to the side of her neck.

As he opened his mouth to lick and suck against her skin, a pleasurable frisson streaked into her erogenous zones. Her lips felt swollen and so did her breasts. Their tips stung. Eddies of need began to swirl in her middle and more intense trickles of excitement grounded like electricity between her legs. She couldn't seem to catch a full breath.

Nor could she think of much else beyond that implacable evidence of his own arousal, undeniable against the back of her hand. He was soothing his fingers up and down her bared spine while his other hand moved to her hip, then traced the crevice of her bottom cheeks through the sequined silk, erotically rubbing the lining of her gown against her skin.

She could hardly breathe; she was so over-whelmed by sensations. She unconsciously cupped her throbbing mons with her hand, try-ing to ease the ache pulsing so insistently there.

"That's mine, Bianca." He nipped her earlobe in small punishment, hand sliding to brush hers aside and replace it. "Do I have to tie your hands behind your back?"

She couldn't answer. Starlight exploded be-hind her eyes as he pushed his hand into the notch of her thighs, palm wide and possessive against her mound. His other arm stayed around her, pinning their arms between them as he said, "Give me your mouth."

She tilted back her head and his mouth cap-tured hers, unceremonious about claiming her. She was fully involved in the flagrant kiss be-fore it had barely started, reveling in the drag-ging heat of his lips across hers, the sweep of his tongue and the flex of his hand between her thighs.

A throaty noise left her, then another. She was growing wet, and she wriggled, needing more pressure. A more purposeful rocking of his hand. She wanted to run her hands over him but was unable to express her desire or to encour-age him except to grind herself into his palm and suck on his tongue.

"Don't peak too early, darling." He loosened the arm that was around her and removed his hand from where he'd been caressing her. "I want you naked and begging when that happens."

"You're a bit of a bastard, aren't you, Everett?" She wasn't joking.

"I'm a lot of a bastard," he assured her as he worked the gown's fitted bodice off her breasts and nudged it down her hips.

The weight of the sequins dragged the fabric into a stiff circle on the floor. She wore only her strapless bra and a pair of matching pink knickers. He made short work of them and helped her step out of the gown.

Now she was naked, forced to stand there as he took his time looking her over. He used one bent knuckle to draw a light circle around her nipple. It was stiff with arousal and bright pink at the tip while the rest of her areola was a pinkish beige. The caress was so light as to be disappointing but made her sex pulse and release another rush of dampness.

He touched her shoulder in a silent urge for her to turn. She did and his hot hand cupped her bottom. "Why are you bruised here?"

The harshness in his tone jolted through her lassitude, making her stiffen.

"I don't rememb— Oh. You scared me. In the garage. I bumped into the mirror of your car."

"Be more careful. Cars can be fixed. You can't." He lightly caressed what had to be a fading yellow mark, then shocked her by kneeling and clasping his arm around her waist as he bent to kiss it better.

She reeled, almost losing her balance, but he straightened and dragged her backward into his chest. His fingers sought the tangled hair of her mound and she felt the rumble of gratification when he discovered her folds were slippery and plump.

She wanted to say she could do that herself, but she couldn't speak. She could only shake and groan with abject need that emanated from the pit of her belly, where the fire he stoked was dancing upward. She rolled her head against his shoulder, nearly mindless with desire as he teased and tantalized, grazing the best spots, but refusing to settle in to properly appease her.

"Everett," she moaned with a pang of frustration.

His caress slowed, drawing out each sensation. "What do you want, lovely?"

"You."

"You're not really in charge here," he reminded, forcing her to endure his lazy caress a little longer. When she was biting her lip, straining for the release she longed for, he eased his touch up her belly, bracing her as she tried to catch her breath. "Have you seen a naked man before, sweet thing?"

She almost said, *Of course. You.*

But this was a game, she recalled. None of it was real, even though she felt truly vulnerable and aroused and very much at his mercy. Of which he seemed to have none.

She had never been so caught up in a need for sex. Wanton craving had her watching him as he unbuttoned his shirt and pulled it from his trousers.

Her reactions were the furthest thing from pretend. She was nearly overcome by the sight of his strong shoulders and wide chest. Oh, she ached to cling and press her mouth against him and taste the salt of his skin. To lick at his abdomen and kiss across his washboard abs. She recalled far too well how his flat hips and those firmly muscled thighs had felt when she straddled them.

And that. His erection. Thick and dark. He slid his hand over and around, comfortable and unabashed as he stroked himself.

"Have you ever touched a man like this? Tasted?" he asked with wicked interest. "Give me what I want, and I may be persuaded to give you what you want."

She flashed her disbelieving gaze up to his. Did he realize she wasn't actually a virgin?

"You'll have to untie me." She was trying for

defiant, but her voice was papery and thick with excitement.

"I don't think so." He sat on the edge of the bed and dropped back onto his elbows, knees splayed. "Take your time."

With a small jab of arrogant I'll-show-him, she sank to her knees between his feet. His eyes gleamed with salacious pleasure.

"Need any tips?" he asked.

"I'll find the one I want when I'm ready," she said tartly, pleased by the wolfish flash of his teeth.

She found a convenient bed rail ledge to balance herself and tilted her head so her hair fell against his inner thigh. She swept it back and forth across his leg, then turned her head and did the other.

His breath deepened and rattled in his chest.

She blew softly all over the flesh before her, then gave him a few dampening licks before doing it again.

His next noise was a deeper inhale, one that seemed a little more pained. His erection bobbed in reaction. She privately smiled and took her time painting him with longer, more licentious licks, offering hot and cool breaths in between. She waited until she heard a curse escape his gritted teeth before she enveloped *just* the tip in the fullness of her mouth.

His eyes closed and he released a guttural groan toward the ceiling.

She drew on him with firm purpose, smiling around the salty flesh that filled her mouth, rather liking the idea of bringing him off this way and getting the better of him when he was being so domineering.

As his tension increased and his breath grated with strain, his eyes snapped open. His hand arrived on her crown. "Stop."

Slowly she released him and brought the back of her wrist to her mouth to dry the dampness from her lips. "Did I do something wrong?"

"You know what you were doing. You think I'll let you control me, Bianca? You really are new to this, aren't you?" He sat up and cradled the back of her head as he plundered her mouth with a burning kiss, tongue thrusting between her lips, letting her know exactly what he wanted to do to her.

She was on her knees before him, helpless. Not from any force on his part, but from the inferno inside her.

When her thoughts were scattered all over again, he broke the kiss and cupped her elbows to help her rise, staying seated on the bed.

She was barely able to make her knees lock, muscles trembling with acute arousal.

"Tell me where you want my mouth. Here?" He pressed his lips to her forearm, then nuzzled his questing mouth across her stomach in the frame of her crossed wrists. His brow brushed the swell of her breast, but he didn't make any effort to find her nipple. He kept up those teasing kisses in innocuous places while his touch traced patterns on the backs of her thighs, down to her knees and up to the round curve of her behind.

"Everett," she begged.

"Are you so new to this you don't know what to ask for?" He drew her closer and made her bend so he could touch his mouth to her breastbone, branding the spot before tipping a look up at her. "Or are you too shy to say it? Show me."

Was he toying with her, or did he really want her to ask? Either way, it made her feel very defenseless when she twisted enough to touch her nipple to the seam of his lips. His hands on her arms firmed. He scraped his damp tongue across the taut bud and drew it into his mouth.

Her body shook. A helpless noise throbbed in her throat as lines of fire went from her swollen breasts to her center. Her sex felt heavy and dewy, ripe with need. It was almost too much, but she couldn't get away, not when his hot hands held her arms like this.

When his mouth released her nipple, she turned like a flower to the sun, giving him the other, lost to that thrum inside her that sought a hidden culmination. It remained frustratingly out of reach. Her inner muscles were clenching on emptiness. An anguished noise left her.

He tipped back his head. "Can you come like this?"

She shook her head, too inflamed to think of her role or anything beyond what he was doing to her. "No. I need you inside me for that. Please, Everett."

There was a hot, primitive flash behind his eyes, though. "Since you asked so nicely." He rose before her. "Stay right here."

She watched him disappear into the bathroom. When he came back, he wore a condom.

He retook his seat on the edge of the bed and motioned her forward, drawing her bound wrists over his head. She braced her elbows on his shoulders as he brought her to straddle his thighs.

"Slowly now. I don't want to hurt you." He gripped his erection in one hand and splayed his other on her hip to guide her. "You're still new to this and I have plans for the rest of the night."

She would have taken him in a greedy drop of her hips, but he kept his fist in the way, encircled around his member, allowing only his crown to fill her. She groaned at the exquisite torture of it.

"Hurt?"

"No. Everett, *please*. Stop teasing." She pressed

her mouth to the side of his throat, sucking a mark there out of sheer frustration.

"Look at me, Bianca."

She picked up her head and forced her heavy eyelids to open.

"Don't look away. I want to watch as you accept that you're mine."

That didn't feel like part of the game.

His touch shifted and now he was allowing her to sink onto him, to feel his full length driving up into her. Stretching and filling. She was the one claiming him, she thought abstractly, but no, he was taking her as surely as if he had her on her back.

He shifted his hand to slide his thumb where they were joined. He stroked her sensitized flesh, circling where her most intense sensations gathered.

Climax was upon her in one, giant pulse, fogging her gaze and spearing intense sensations upward and outward. She was both melting and catching fire. Exploding and dissolving.

"Eyes open, lovely. Oh, that's beautiful."

She might have had her eyes open. All she saw was piercing blue and glittering stars. Powerful ripples rolled through her abdomen and joy shimmered into her extremities. Her lax mouth couldn't form words, but her throat was making trembling noises of ecstasy.

"Yes," he crooned, holding her hips tight in

his lap while the waves went on and on. "Now you're mine, aren't you? All mine."

She was. Deep, deep in her soul. No other man would ever take her apart so tenderly, then put her back together with those smooth hands sliding across her back, encircling her in the safety of his embrace.

But he wasn't hers. He was still hard inside her, his self-discipline almost terrifying, it was so unbreakable.

As her orgasm faded and her breath began to even out, he kissed her chin. "Do you know what happens now, my darling?"

She couldn't imagine.

"You lie back and think of *me* while I show you all the other ways you belong to me."

The explosion was six blocks away, but it shook the floor of the fleabag apartment Everett stood in. He ran for the stairs, not frightened for himself. No, he knew what had happened and it was his fault. He even knew that he was already too late, but he had to get there. Had to stop it from happening.

Outside, the air was thick as molasses. No matter how hard he pumped his arms and legs, they were heavy as concrete. Useless. He couldn't get himself down the street.

A lucid part of his brain knew this was a dream, that his struggle was futile, but he still tried. He had to get there. Had to prevent it. To undo what shouldn't have happened.

In a whoosh he was standing next to the overturned wheelchair, its wheels bent. The man who used it was thrown facedown next to it. His body, already ravaged once by a horrific accident, had been damaged again. Because of him.

"Everett."

Freja? She shouldn't be here.

She was rattling his shoulder, hating him. Hating him so intensely for what he'd done, but no one could hate him as much as he hated himself.

"Everett, wake *up*."

His dream vanished and his eyes snapped open. His cotton-filled head was still in Dubrovnik, slow to catch up to his body in Miami.

He was in the bed of the hotel suite. Bianca was running her hand up and down his arm, crooning, "It's okay, it's okay."

He was coated in clammy sweat that turned to a blanket of self-contempt.

Damn it, why hadn't he realized this might happen? The replays always happened when he slept hard, and damned if he hadn't fallen into a near coma after wringing both of them dry with energetic lovemaking.

"Were you having a nightmare? Your heart is racing."

He brushed her caressing hand from his

chest and mopped the edge of the sheet across his torso.

"Do you want to talk about it?" she asked with concern.

"No. Go back to sleep." He swung his legs off the side of the bed, doubtful he'd fall asleep again. Not for hours and not next to her. This was his own private hell and a well-deserved recompense for what he'd nearly done.

Her soft palm moved across his lower back. Her touch was meant to comfort, but it had the effect of reawakening his libido. How? That thing ought to have been run to death by now, but nope. He only had to recall how her thighs had clamped his ears and he was seriously considering a fresh seduction as pure distraction, but he would only fall asleep again and they'd be right back here.

He rose to pull on his pants.

"Where are you going?"

"I need a minute." He didn't look at her because he would only want to crawl back into bed with her.

In the lounge, he poured himself a double Scotch and stood at the window, noting stragglers at the bar by the pool, still partying despite the glow of pale gold condensing on the horizon.

He shouldn't have made love to her. So much for prom rules.

On the other hand, he was only human. When

she had suggested taking things upstairs, his self-control had only extended to ensuring she was going into this with realistic expectations.

He'd thought playing out a fantasy would be less intimate, but oddly, it was more. It had forced both of them to reveal deeper aspects of themselves while trusting the other more fully. She had had to believe she was safe with him. He had put his faith in her calling a halt if he came on too strong.

He had reveled in his role. Letting himself imagine he was the only man to ever touch her, the only man who could make her scream in the throes of orgasm, was a kink he hadn't known was in him, but there it was. He hadn't been able to get enough of her. He'd touched and tasted every part of her, made her shake and moan and say, 'Please.'

In the end, he'd been so desperate for his own culmination, he'd pleaded with her to join him. *Once more, love. You can do it. Come with me. Let me feel it.*

She'd been flushed and glowing, lips swollen from their kisses, eyes unfocused as she arched beneath him. A fantasy come to life and the fantasy had been that she was *his*. Forever.

As the fine quivers of her sheath had begun to ripple around his thrusts, all the mutual caresses and kisses and strokes of pleasure that had piled up like sticks of dynamite had detonated.

He had sheltered her beneath him as the shock waves of orgasm shuddered through them. So many sensations had accosted him then—her soft body cushioning his, her crashing heart-beat against his own, her ecstatic cries and the clenching heat that matched his own pulsing release. Their voices had combined in ragged cries of ecstasy.

He had felt as though he had left a vital piece of himself inside her after he withdrew, even though he'd worn a condom. Whatever small shield that thin wall had afforded didn't extend to his psyche. He'd been the most unguarded of his life in those moments and he hadn't wanted to pick apart how he could feel so much more than the amiable gratitude he usually experienced after sex. He was always satisfied and thankful to his partner for sharing her body, but much like his first time with Bianca, he had been aware of a nagging sensation of *not enough*.

What would it take? he wondered. At this rate, they'd do themselves an injury trying to satiate their desire for one another.

There was a clink behind him. He turned to see Bianca pouring herself a glass of Scotch. She wore a hotel robe, and her face was freshly washed, all traces of makeup gone.

She curled up in the corner of the sofa and sipped carefully, eyes on the contents of her glass.

"I don't want to talk about it," he told her.

"I don't expect you to. Sometimes it's nice to have someone sit with you when you're troubled, though."

The way he and Giovanni had sat with each other? The guilt that always dogged him caught up enough to nip at him.

He heaved a sigh at the ceiling, but the weight stayed on his chest. It belonged there. And it wasn't as if he hadn't talked about it to his superiors. When you nearly killed your best operative, you had to answer for it.

But his colleagues had all said, *You did what you had to*, as if that was a good enough excuse.

That's not what Bianca would say. She would be rightfully horrified and disgusted. She would berate him and give him the contempt he deserved.

"Giovanni worked for me," he said. "Technically. He's not the sort who needs a lot of direction, and the nature of the work doesn't lend itself to performance metrics. It was more of a partnership, but it was my responsibility to determine if he was fit for the things I was asking him to do. I could see he wasn't, but I let him continue anyway."

"Drugs?" she asked with astonishment.

"No," he snorted. "No, he was falling in love with Freja. Losing his focus. Shifting it, is a better word. Freja was becoming his priority. He didn't want to admit it. Not to me, not to her. Not even to himself," he said in dry recollection. "He swore she wasn't affecting his ability to be objective. I'd always trusted him, so I continued to trust him. I should have listened to my gut."

His chest was lined with spikes that were digging deeper on each heavy breath he took. He stopped short of revealing that Freja had been pregnant at the time. Her pregnancy and the loss of it were too personal to relay, but it added countless layers of anguish to the remorse Everett still carried.

"What happened?" Bianca asked softly.

"Giovanni was planning to retire, but he wanted to finish a job we were working on. That sort of work isn't something where you just promote someone else into a position. You have to take time, build trust. Even doing it myself would have set everything back months. That could have cost lives, but he was rushing things, trying to hurry a meeting. It literally blew up. He was nearly killed."

She gasped. "I saw something online about him being thought dead for a while. I couldn't find any details, though."

"It's all been scrubbed, but yes, declaring him dead was my decision," he said grimly. "I was protecting him from further attack, but that meant I had to let Freja believe it."

"That her husband was *dead*? You did that

to her? But they love each other *so much*. That was really cruel, Everett." She was appalled and there was no satisfaction in hearing it.

"It was cruel," he agreed. Especially when she lost her baby and they couldn't be together. That's why Everett could barely look at himself in the mirror. That's why he couldn't accept that they still valued his friendship.

"But you did what you could to make it up to her," she recalled. "Freja said you put yourself in hospital to get a message to her foster mother."

"What I should have done was take Giovanni out of the field before it even happened. I knew something was off that day. Call it experience, call it intuition. I knew I shouldn't let him work, but I didn't stop him, and I should have."

"We all make mistakes, Everett."

"Not the kind that cost lives!" He rounded on her, refusing to accept any quarter. "Not the kind that causes months of suffering. If you had seen him in the hospital, wanting to get to her." His voice grew ragged, and he was right back to trembling in the aftermath of his nightmare. Back to trembling beside his best friend's broken body. He was a monster and deserved to be exiled to the farthest reaches of the universe for what he'd done. "If he hadn't been in traction, he would have crawled out to find her." He ran his hand down his face, trying to erase that day, that awful day when he had had to tell Giovanni that the baby was gone.

"Is that what the nightmare is about?" she asked gently. "The explosion?"

"Yes. It happens when I sleep too hard. I know he's about to be ambushed, I want to keep him from going to the café, but I can't get to him in time."

"Did you know that he was about to be ambushed?"

"Of course not." He brought his head up and scowled at her. "I never would have sent him into that. It was supposed to be a conversation with an informant, but I shouldn't have let him go to Dubrovnik at all."

"Because your instinct told you not to."

"Yes. And it never lets me down. It told me not to get involved with you, and look what happened when I ignored it then." That was a cheap swipe because he was feeling so damned exposed. Because she was being kind instead of hating him the way he wanted her to.

Her breath left her as though she'd taken a kick to the stomach. The tendons in her neck flexed before she lifted her glass and drank.

And that just made him feel worse. "I shouldn't have said that."

"It's fine," she said in a voice seared thin by the burn of alcohol. "It's not like we're the kind of lovers who are mindful of each other's feelings."

His breath left him at the effortless way she delivered a body blow equal to his, but he had to admire that streak of toughness beneath her kitten-soft appearance.

"I think you should apologize to them," she declared.

"They know I'm sorry."

"You should apologize and ask for their forgiveness and let them forgive you." She drained her glass and leaned to set it on the coffee table. "The way you're pushing them away hurts them. Is that something you want to do? Continue to hurt them?"

"No," he grumbled.

"Then stop. Maybe the nightmares will stop, too." She rose. "I'm going back to bed. Good night."

I didn't ask for advice, he wanted to gripe, but the door closed without an invitation for him to join her. *Big surprise*, he thought ironically and turned his face back to the window. He'd been a complete ass.

He released a sigh that fogged the glass.

If Everett had come back to bed in the wee hours, he left before she woke.

Bianca was thankful. She wasn't ready to face him after their predawn exchange. It was true that she'd been a hurricane-level disaster in his life, but it had still hurt to hear how much he begrudged her for it, especially when she had gone out to him because she was worried about him. His nightmare had been causing his whole body to thrash, which was what had woken her. His breathing had been ragged, his face in the pale light tortured.

After everything they had shared in this bed, she had been compelled to try to comfort him. She had been touched that he entrusted her with what was a deeply personal and painful experience. She had thought it was a sign of closeness and had wanted to support him and help him work through it.

Then he had made that nasty remark, reminding her that all they shared was biology. Their lovemaking had not built an emotional connection. It had been a fantasy. Not real.

Which left her hollowed out and chilled despite a hot shower and a bright, sunny day.

She was still physically tender and emotionally exposed as she dressed, thinking of how much of herself she had shared. Yes, they'd started out playing a part, but the line had soon blurred. The pleasure of his touch, of feeling him against her and within her, had been very real. They had still been *them*. Hadn't they?

She had, but when she thought of it in the starkness of daylight, she didn't see where he had been anything more than titillated by their game. When he had suffered a moment of vulnerability, telling her the cause of his nightmare, he had lashed out right after, cutting off any more expressions of empathy.

Realizing how ruthlessly he could shut her out galvanized her into putting her own defenses back into place, otherwise she would suffer more than this sense of scorn in the time they were together. She would get her heart shattered.

She combed out her damp hair and put on a little makeup, then found Everett at the table on the balcony, pouring coffee.

"Good morning." She tried for a breezy tone, but his circumspect glance was enough to wash her in a fresh wave of vulnerability.

Aside from the dark circles around his eyes, he was his clean-shaven, sharply dressed self, but *she* knew how those masculine lips felt against her skin, how those strong hands could guide and caress. She knew he was both demanding and generous, powerful yet tender. She knew that *he* knew she couldn't refuse him anything.

"I heard you in the shower and took the liberty of ordering." He set aside the carafe and lifted the lids from the plates. Both held lobster Benedict with tomato and asparagus, fresh fruit and a small crepe rolled around a berry compote.

There was no particular warmth in his greeting. No sexy lingering glance or a sly *Sleep well*? Not even anything to suggest regrets over their talk, just a shuttered expression and that scrupulously polite tone.

She wasn't sure what reaction she had expected, but it wasn't this complete detachment, as if their lovemaking hadn't happened at all.

Biting her lips together to keep them from trembling, she sat, but her usually healthy appetite dried up. She refused to ask if everything was all right. She refused to be needy. This was exactly why her mother had instilled in her to hold herself apart from emotional dependence on a man. *Your worth is determined by you, not bestowed by anyone else.*

"The Catalanos will be here in a moment. They wanted to say goodbye before they fly to New York."

"Oh. Good." Her brain couldn't seem to catch up to his crisp, businesslike attitude. "Freja asked me why I was doing so many of my interviews and depositions here instead of there. I told her I didn't know." There were both a criminal and a class action civil suit being brought against Morris and Ackerley, not to mention a metric ton of media interest and a congressional committee hearing on how the scheme had gone undetected for so long. Miami wasn't the most convenient place for providing statements and evidence to any of those.

"That was my call. It made sense at the time."

"In what way?" She chased a blueberry with the tine of her fork.

"Inconveniencing Ackerley's people, mostly." He ate a morsel of lobster. "They'll be billing as much for travel as they do for legal services."

"Do I want to antagonize him like that?"

"I do."

"Why?"

"Because I don't like him."

She would have probed that remark, but she heard the ping of a doorbell. She rose to invite the Catalanos into the suite.

Everett followed her in, and Bianca executed a somewhat passive-aggressive move by saying, "Girls, help me count the people in the pool. You can teach me to do it in Sicilian."

She took them by the hands and pointedly closed the glass door behind them, locking Everett inside with Giovanni and Freja.

Fifteen minutes later, Freja came out with wet lashes and a big, trembling smile. She hugged Bianca extra hard.

"Thank you," she breathed. "We're not staying in New York more than a few days, but *please* come visit us in Sicily."

"If I'm allowed to leave the country, sure." It was a joke, but not entirely.

"Giovanni can help if you need it. But I'm serious. No matter what happens with Everett, you and I are friends now. I want you to come."

Moved, Bianca nodded, and they went inside where Giovanni waved her to bend so he could hug her and kiss both her cheeks.

"You'll come see us in Sicily," he informed her. "Soon. Let me know when you're free. I'll arrange it."

"I will," she promised, and waved the family off, heart full at seeing them so happy.

Then she apprehensively looked at Everett, half expecting a thunderous berating for interfering, but he was locked up behind his most inscrutable, flinty expression.

"Are you angry?" she asked.

"I'm going to shower, then we'll head back to the house."

"You're not going to finish your breakfast?"

"It will only taste like crow."

She ate the rest of hers alone.

Was he angry? Everett was still brooding on that hours later when he sat in on a meeting between Bianca and one of the producers from Freja's movie.

The entertainment sharks were circling, looking for the tastiest bite of her story before it was completely written. He'd warned her not to sign anything and was present to ensure they didn't pull a fast one, but he recognized she needed an income, and these sorts of offers could be very generous.

He listened with half an ear to the tedious attempt to seduce her into exploiting her private life. She kept politely rebuffing and they kept upping the ante.

Yes, Everett decided. He was angry, but not in the way she meant. He was angry that she had been right. He was angry that he had continued to hurt his friends without seeing the injury he was doing to them. He was angry that, instead of being an instrument of ruin, the way he wanted to pigeonhole Bianca, she had helped him fix a part of his life that he had broken all by himself.

He was angry that instead of walking around with a stab of righteous self-hatred turning in his gut, he was awash in an ache of humility. Apologizing to Giovanni hadn't been that hard. He had said those words before.

Being forgiven, however, had caused a pain that was not unlike a bone being reset. It still hurt like hell, but it was the dull throb of healing. It made him feel tender and tentative, and he didn't like that at all.

Bianca wasn't being smug about pushing him into reconciling with his friend, either, which would have let him resent her. No, she was holding on to some frost from his snarky comment last night, disappearing to do yoga the minute she got the producer out the door. He didn't see her again until they sat down for dinner, and she was still quiet and withdrawn.

"You were right," he acknowledged. "I should have done that a long time ago, and I'm glad it's not between me and Giovanni any longer. And you have a right to be angry with me about what I said. But it's not that I don't care about your feelings, Bianca. I do. I just don't want them to attach themselves to me."

"Yes, I got that memo," she said, her own voice cool, then easing to something more plaintive. "I'm not angry with you. I'm realizing why you were so angry with me. The way that producer was prying for details on my personal life made me realize how intrusive it is."

The stubble at the back of his neck stood up and his ears crackled. Immediately, his mind replayed the meeting, zeroing in on the way her jaw had grown stubbornly locked when she'd been asked about her absent father.

"We're conditioned to believe we should know our biological parents," he noted. "I was surprised to hear you didn't have any father figure at all in your life. Or were you protecting someone from being hunted down when you told him your mother never married?"

"No, that was true. Mom was a nurse and worked a lot of nights. It wasn't conducive to dating and she didn't want to confuse me with a string of men who might not stick. She was determined to get me through college without loans, too. She worked a ton of overtime."

"You said she never told your father that she was pregnant. Why not?"

"Why should she?" A note of challenge entered her tone, but her voice quavered ever so slightly.

He was standing on a very raw nerve. What was that about?

"To give him a chance to step up?" Everett suggested lightly. "I would certainly like to know if I had a child out there somewhere."

"Would you?" Her spine snapped straight, and her fork went down with a clunk. "What if *I* become pregnant? What do you expect *me* to do?"

His shoulders hit the back of his chair and a churn of gravel arrived in his stomach.

"I expect you not to get pregnant." His teeth hurt, he clenched his jaw so tight. "That's why I wear condoms. I don't want children."

"Mom took precautions, yet here I am." She waved at herself, chiding, "Even fantasies can have consequences, Everett."

His heart was pounding so hard, his lungs were having trouble catching a breath.

"But don't worry," she muttered into the glass she raised. She took a big swallow of wine, then set it down. "Wanting children is a very personal decision. I wouldn't expect anyone to get on board just because I want them. I would deal with it myself."

"How?" The word shot out of him like a bullet.

A flash of shock bloomed behind her eyes.

"I won't know unless it happens, will I?" Her brows went up, but her mouth was trembling. "I would likely continue the pregnancy and raise the child myself. Alone. The way Mom did. It's not easy, but it's not impossible."

"And you wouldn't even tell me? I would want to know, Bianca." His own glass should have shattered in his hand, he was holding it so tightly.

"Why? What would you do?" she challenged.

"I won't know unless it happens," he said caustically. "But I want to know if it does." Ignorance was *not* bliss. It was ignorance. And even though this conversation was hypothetical, the idea she might keep something that profound from him thrust a wedge of deprivation into him.

"Noted." She threw her napkin onto the table and rose. "I'm going for a bath." She took her wine with her.

Bianca couldn't fall asleep. She kept thinking of Everett's emphatic, *I don't want children*. And the fact that the easiest way not to slip up and have a surprise pregnancy would be to not have sex at all.

She threw her arm over her eyes, hating that idea even more than having a child with a reluctant father. She'd been honest about not pressing a man to have a family if he didn't want one, but if that's what he would be, she shouldn't run the risk of pregnancy, should she?

She flipped her pillow to the cool side and stuffed her face into it.

That was only one of many reasons they didn't have a future ahead of them. Her whistleblowing would have repercussions for years. Not only was it unfair to ask him to stand by her through that, but he was underwriting a lot of her support. She had cornered him into that— unwittingly, but she had still done it.

And she hadn't fully appreciated how much he must resent the attention she had put on him until she had begun taking calls for interviews. Most of them had stuck to asking about her relationship with Troy, which was intrusive enough, but that producer today had wanted to do a memoir like Freja's. He had been taking notes about where she went to college and where her mother had worked. When he had asked about her father, Bianca had nearly snapped.

Yet again, she wondered if she should tell Everett who her father was. Warn him. But if she was the only one who knew, how could it affect him? No, as long as she kept it to herself, they were both safe from any ramifications on that front.

The door latch quietly clicked, and she instinctively held very still, trying to calm her breathing so he would think she was asleep.

He went into the bathroom to brush his teeth, and she clenched her eyes shut, willing herself to drop off, but she was still lying there stiff as a board when he slid onto the other side of the mattress. The bed was wider than the Great Plains and so well-made she didn't feel any dip or movement, but she felt his presence all the same.

His tension.

She hadn't moved one iota since he had entered the bedroom, but he said, "I thought you'd be asleep by now."

How was he so perceptive? She rolled onto her back.

"You're basically the most important person in my life right now. I don't like fighting with you," she said.

"Is that really what's keeping you awake? Because it didn't feel like a fight."

It wasn't. Whatever injury she had taken from the conversation had been disappointment that they were so different, not hurt at being attacked.

He clicked on the lamp on his side, then rolled

to prop himself on his elbow, facing her. He was naked from the waist up, usually wearing boxers to bed from the few peeks she'd caught.

"But we could still kiss and make up," he suggested. "At least then we'll be able to sleep."

She rolled her eyes, then asked with mocking sweetness, "Are you sure you want to risk it?"

His face fell into grave lines. The sobriety in his voice left a chill across her skin. "That's why you don't want to have children with me, Bianca. I have a taste for risk that is higher than most can stomach."

He slid closer and loomed over her.

She pressed deeper into the mattress and set her hand on his chest, but he only reached to her night table and picked up the book she'd been reading in the bath. He read the back.

"Forced marriage." He slid her an amused look. "I think we could work with that." He continued to read. "I actually have majority shares in the shipping line that my great-grandfather started so I check the box for shipping magnate. That leaves you and what you're prepared to do for your grandmother's farmhouse." He set the book aside and held himself over her with his arms on either side of her. "Will you consummate this marriage?" His nose nuzzled hers. "It's in the will that we have to treat it as a *real* marriage."

He was big and solid, and his breath smelled

like mint. The fine hairs on his chest were teasing her fingertips to pet him. If she did, she would bump into the hard bead of his nipple, and she really wanted to do that. She wanted to make his breath hiss and feel his body tremble and hear him call her *Mine*.

It's just a game. Harmless fun, she reasoned.

She turned her face to the side. "I'll submit to my conjugal duty, but I won't remove my nightgown."

"Oh? Why's that?"

"Scars. My grandmother believed I was too fearful of rejection to marry anyone. That's why she made this condition that I marry. Turn out the light."

"I've seen a lot in my rough life. I think I can handle it." His lips brushed hers.

She jerked her face to the side again. "And no kissing on the mouth. My grandparents fell in love the first time they kissed. I don't want to fall in love with you."

He stilled for one pulsebeat, then drawled, "Lie back and let me have my way, then. I'll try not to bother you too much."

His mouth went into the crook of her neck while his hand searched beneath the covers, finding the hem of her nightgown and caressing the tops of her thighs.

She slid her arms over his shoulders and sifted her fingers into his hair, instinctually wanting to draw him to kiss her, but his tickling touch found her tangle of damp curls.

He made a rough noise of pleased discovery. "You have been lying here waiting for me, haven't you?"

She had. Shimmering pleasure swept through her pelvis as he casually pressed her legs apart and fondled her with a more proprietary touch.

"Poor neglected wife. Don't worry. I'll make it good for you." He set small kisses across her jawline as he swirled her dampness over her folds, parting and easily sliding one finger, then two, into her.

She groaned and dipped her chin to search for his mouth, but he shifted so he could find her nipple through the fabric of her nightgown. His hot mouth dampened the silk, and he used his tongue to rub it against the distended button.

Tension gathered across her abdomen. She instinctually lifted her hips, encouraging the rocking caress of his hand, clamping down as he found a spot that made stars appear behind her clenched eyelids. Very suddenly she was bucking in sharp, heady climax.

He was saying something to her in a gratified voice and slowed his caress to draw out her pleasure. She couldn't hear it through her shaken moans of joy.

His mouth came back to her neck and her cheek and her brow before he finally eased his touch away.

"You do want that farmhouse, don't you, darling? Will you do anything I ask?" He threw off the covers and dragged a pillow into the middle of the bed. "Let's try this."

She was still trembling with the final shivers of climax, muscles too lax to do anything but cooperate as he rolled her stomach onto the pillows and positioned her knees under her.

He kicked off his boxers and applied a condom, then brushed her nightgown up her buttocks, exposing her as he sought her still-molten entrance. He pressed into her, the wide dome of his erection forging where his fingers had been, reaching deeper, filling her more completely.

She closed her fists into the sheets, groaning at how good it felt to have him inside her.

When his hips were flat against her buttocks, he bent to cover her and kissed her neck and licked her ear. Then he dragged her hand down between her own thighs and said, "Let me feel it this time. Make yourself come again."

She couldn't deny him anything. He straightened and took hold of her hips, thrusting with steady power while she caressed herself and bit her lip and arrived at the crisis with embarrassing speed, practically screaming her sharp release into the mattress.

She could have wept, he made her feel so good.

He folded onto her again, crooning noises of approval and gratitude as he palmed her breast and suckled her earlobe. Carefully, he withdrew and rolled her onto her back, then slid inside her again, catching her up in his arms and drawing her into his lap as he rose to kneel on the bed.

"Do you know what kills me, Bianca?"

She clung to his shoulders and dragged her eyes open. "What?" Her lips were buzzing and her brain was too far away to imagine anything could bother either of them right now.

"That I left you to do that for yourself all those months when I could have been right here—" His hand flattened on her tailbone, and he shifted so he penetrated a fraction deeper. "Helping you, the whole time."

Her heart juddered to a halt in her chest.

Those words meant too much. They suggested things. They made her think she'd been on his mind the way he'd been on hers. They made her think he had missed her while they were apart and would later, when they were no longer together.

She didn't want to think of that. It made a scalded sensation rise in the back of her throat, one that burned all the way into the center of her being.

"I thought we only met and married this morning."

The piercing blue of his eyes reflected fiery heat and arctic ice.

She held her breath until his mouth curled into a self-deprecating line.

"Am I ruining the fantasy? Let me make it up to you." He eased her onto her back and began to thrust, sending her back into that golden place where nothing mattered but the fact they were joined. No longer two disjointed people, but one perfect entity. Whole.

She ran her hands over the landscape of his shoulders and back and buttocks, claiming all of him while she had the chance. He hooked his arm under one of her legs and drove deeper, making her writhe at the intensity of the sensations.

"There, Everett. There. Don't stop." She was straining for the pinnacle, hands going into his hair again, so she cradled his skull. "Never stop."

"Never," he vowed, muscles bunched as he thrust hard and fast, bringing her with him as he raced toward climax.

There it was. The horizon where she would tip off into the sun. He was right there with her, gritting through his teeth, "Now, Bee, now."

As the quaking fracture tore across the earth toward them, he clamped his mouth over hers in a hot, passionate, claiming kiss.

They fell.

CHAPTER EIGHT

"SERIOUSLY, LOOK AT these two," Bianca said a week later when they were in the car. "Freja doesn't want me to go to Sicily. I'll kidnap her children and bring them home with me."

Everett glanced at the photo of Louisa and Theresa caught playing dress-up with Freja's sunglasses, jewelry, handbags and oversize shoes.

"Cute," he pronounced, because he wasn't a sociopath, but if Bianca was hoping for him to wax poetic with adoration and suggest they make a set of their own, she would be sorely disappointed.

"They are," she agreed. She turned off her phone and dropped it into her handbag, then turned her nose to the window.

She was disappointed. His conscience pinched.

Even fantasies can have consequences, Everett.

He kept thinking of that and how his brain

had flatlined at the thought of her pregnant. Her suggestion of raising his child alone—*Don't worry about it*—had gone against every sense of decency he possessed.

He had gone to bed that night thinking, fine, they wouldn't have sex anymore. The chance of making a baby was one risk too far for even his nearly infinite threshold. He was still scarred from having to tell Giovanni that Freja had lost their first pregnancy. He could hardly bear recalling it, let alone contemplate experiencing it himself. He sure as hell wouldn't want to be responsible for Bianca going through that.

But when he got into bed, she'd been awake. The pull between them had been impossible to resist. He didn't *want* to control his desire for her. That was the problem. He wanted to revel in it no matter how self-destructive it might prove to be.

If she had stopped him, he would have backed off, but she had gone along with it. He'd never met a woman so greedy for orgasms. It made him want to spend all day, every day, giving them to her.

A review of their track record revealed he'd spent a week doing exactly that. Between meetings and social engagements, he'd been an Australian station owner, brushed up on his Greek for an island stranding, seduced his winemaker on his Chilean vineyard and skipped the step-brother role in favor of being her brother's best friend holding a grudge over a broken career. An hour ago, he had been her ex-husband snowed in with her at their Whistler chalet.

When he had asked her why she read romance over anything else, she had said, "They keep me company, like friends. I lost touch with most of my real ones while Mom was sick. I made a few at work, but once I started gathering evidence, I was afraid I'd slip up if I went out for drinks with any of them. And they all had lives. Careers and marriage and families. I was taking a hatchet to my chances for all of that, so I insulated myself. I like that romance takes me out of the crater where my life used to be, and they always end happily, which gives me hope. I need that. It's really hard being alone."

Which was why she wanted a family.

That always put an ache in the pit of his stomach, but he had always thought of it the other way. It was really hard to care about someone. You worried for them. Hurt for them. He still had his mother, but she was thankfully healthy and lived a quiet life that caused him very little anguish. He cared about Giovanni and his family, but the worst of the responsibility for their welfare fell on his friend. Still, if something happened to any of them, Everett would be gutted.

There was a difference between preferring to

stand on the sidelines of life and being pushed there by circumstance, though. Bianca obviously wanted to throw herself into that emotionally messy fray, foolishly brave soul that she was.

She couldn't have that with him, though, and maybe he owed her the real reason why.

"My father wanted more children. My mother refused." He ran his hand over his thigh, never finding it pleasant to talk about his childhood. "I think she wanted them, but my father was difficult to live with. She was afraid he wouldn't be there for her."

"Because of the brain injury?"

"Even before that. He got into automotive engineering because he loved speed. Any high-risk activity, really. That was really distressing for my mother, never knowing if he would come home."

"I've never understood how anyone gets a thrill out of being in danger. The whole time I was sneaking around behind Troy's back, my stomach was in knots." She rolled her lips inward before giving a small snort. "That doesn't bother you, though. Does it? The fear of getting caught."

It bothered him right now, when he glanced into her soft brown eyes and knew she saw straight into his soul. His chest felt unguarded. Exposed.

"It's a common misconception that daredevils

are impulsive idiots with no sense of self-preservation. Some are, but my father was actually a control junkie. He believed he could anticipate all the risks and calculate all the variables and triumph over the fragility of being human."

"And you?" She already knew. He'd told her his tolerance for risk was more than she could stomach.

"I was blessed with his nature, and he nurtured it." His mouth twisted with self-deprecation. "I was seven when he first took me out onto a test track. He got us up to two hundred miles an hour. I freaking loved it."

"That's more than dangerous, isn't it?" she gasped. "I'm no physicist, but aren't there g-forces or something that would kill a small child?"

"If he had stopped and started too abruptly, yes. That's why my mother lost her mind over it. The more I followed in his tire tracks, the more she withdrew from both of us. To this day, she'll claim that she sent me to boarding school so she could be more accessible at work, but I think she was keeping me from seeing how distressed she was."

"That's sad." She studied him. "I'm sorry, Everett. That must have been very painful."

He shrugged it off. "People do what they have to, to protect themselves. Part of the reason I emulated him was a twisted attempt not to fear for him. If I could survive racing a car through Monte Carlo, he could survive whatever he was doing, despite catching fire on a closed track. My mother didn't have that outlook. She couldn't bear the tension and told him she wanted a divorce. That was right before he crashed."

"He crashed because he was upset?"

"Maybe. But I'm not saying the crash was her fault. You shouldn't punch the gas on eight hundred and fifty horsepower if your mind is elsewhere," he said crisply. "And if you don't want to take your family into consideration before you do things like that, then don't have one."

That was the crux of it.

She nodded solemnly. "I see your point, but you don't do those high-risk things."

"I want to. I took a job where I nearly got my best friend killed. I swore off doing that work and less than a year later, I'm rolling around with a white-collar whistleblower, leaving myself susceptible to my secret life coming to light. I'm not a good bet, Bianca. You don't *want* me as a father for your children. I don't want to father children and be *that* father."

She looked straight ahead. In the flash of streetlights, he thought he saw a glimmer of dampness on her eyes. "That's what you meant when you called me a gateway drug and said your instinct told you not to get involved with me."

"I wasn't trying to be cruel. Hell, much of my desire to take risks is fueled by a hero complex. From the minute I realized what sort of enemy you had pitted yourself against, I wanted to back you up. It's arrogant, but I get off on getting the better of bad guys."

It hadn't been purely a white knight instinct, though. No, from the moment he'd looked across at her in the jet that day, he had wanted to know what was going on behind her alluring expression. His body responded to her, yes. Powerfully. But his mind was equally engaged. She fascinated him and challenged him and from those first moments, she had set a ticking clock inside him. He had decided long ago he would never marry anyone, never subject his own family to the fraught years he had suffered through, but there had been an urgency within him when he met her. They had a limited time, but he wanted to learn everything about her in the time they had.

"What happened with your father?" she asked. "Your parents didn't reconcile after his crash?"

"They tried. Mom blamed herself. My father couldn't get it out of his head that she hadn't wanted him when he was fully fit. How could she want him now? He wasn't capable of performing the sorts of calculations that had allowed him to excel in his field, so his career was over. He drank a lot, started having affairs. Eventually, they divorced. Dad's health deteriorated and he died from a heart attack a few years ago."

"I'm sorry, Everett."

"It was the consequence of living the way he did. That's why I don't want to lead you on. We won't live happily ever after, Bianca."

"I'm not a child, Everett," she said frostily. "I know happiness is fleeting. But you still have to chase it on the off chance you can catch hold of it for a minute or two. If you've already written off even trying to be happy, then yes, you're right. We don't have a chance and should probably quit while we're ahead."

"How did you and Everett meet?" a woman asked Bianca.

"I—" Shoot. That was a new one.

Bianca's mind was still on their altercation in the car. It sounded like Everett had had a difficult childhood where he identified with a man who had destroyed himself while his mother withheld her love for fear her son was turning out the same. She didn't blame Everett for being wary of repeating history with his own child, but his bleak view of things had laid waste to the tiny sprouts of hope she'd allowed to form.

All of that meant she felt terribly obvious when she sent a look of besotted adoration up to him, but her mind had gone completely blank. "Do you want to tell her, darling?"

He'd been wearing a remote mask. It smoothed into something more urbane.

"Bianca sat next to me on a plane," he replied without hesitation. "I couldn't take my eyes off her." His hand possessively came to rest at the small of her back. "She met me for dinner and moved into my home a few weeks later."

A pang struck her chest at how sweetly he reframed the truth into something that actually sounded as though they were smitten with one another.

This was how it went with every new couple or group they met. Bianca would try to remember that none of this was real, then Everett would touch her, and her body's reaction was *very* real. Her nerve endings came alive, and the rich timbre of his voice seemed to resonate in her chest. He would look at her a certain way and, for a few precious seconds, she would feel valued and desired and necessary.

"That's not as cute as I hoped." The senator's wife pouted in disappointment before an avid light came into her eyes. "But then you eloped, didn't you? Was that because you were hiding from the press? Or your fiancé?"

This was also how it went. They had a moment of accord, then reality smacked her in the face like a wet rag, reminding her why Everett was bothering to put on this charade.

Bianca smiled, pretending to find the remark as funny as the woman did, but Everett stiffened.

"We eloped because we're private people," Everett said bluntly. "Excuse us. I see someone I need to speak with." He led Bianca into the crush.

"That was rude," Bianca chided.

"Yes, she was."

Bianca had been talking about his behavior, but he wasn't wrong. That woman had been overstepping. She was hardly the first one, though.

They had fallen into a pattern where they sat in meetings all day with consultants and lawyers and advisors. Bianca carefully filtered every word she spoke and tried not to snap in half from the tension.

Then they would have an hour or two to themselves and always made love madly, dressing it up so it wasn't them. It was a part they played. A game. An excuse for her to lose herself in his touch and pretend she was keeping the most susceptible parts of herself protected.

That was the biggest lie in all of this because she was falling in love with him. How could she not? He was smart and sexy and protective. Passionate and wry and honest.

He was the man she wanted to father her children, but he didn't want to be that man so she would rise from the bed and pretend it had been nothing more than a bit of fun. She would truss herself into a designer gown so Everett could parade her around a dinner or gala. Most nights she didn't mind it. She could allow her true feelings for him to radiate out of her in what was probably the most unfiltered hours of her day.

Tonight, after how things had gone in the car, she couldn't reveal herself in that same way. She was peeled so raw, the judgy looks from people who were being fed lies by Troy and his ilk stabbed especially deep. According to Troy, Bianca was both a cheating fiancée and a scorned lover who had manufactured evidence to harm Morris and Ackerley. No one believed she was merely a woman who had exposed wrongdoing because her conscience demanded it.

It made for an interminable night, one where she felt more lonely and forsaken, surrounded by people with Everett's hand enfolding hers, than she had in the time before he had crashed back into her life.

She was tempted to drink herself into a stupor, but since she had to be so cautious in what she said at these things, she only ever carried a half-full wineglass around, barely tasting a drop. Therefore, she didn't really need the ladies' room when she said, "Can I catch up to you in a minute? I need the powder room."

"Of course. Look for me near those windows. There's a man I'd like to speak to over there."

She nodded and hurried away, desperate for a break from the unrelenting tension of soaking in Everett's sex appeal while knowing his courtly gestures were only pandering to their audience. He was never going to feel about her the way she felt about him.

The attendant in the powder room was doing a brisk business in hemming and manicure triage, but she offered Bianca a glass of ice water that Bianca used to wash down a capsule for her dull headache. She lingered to fiddle with her hair and makeup, wondering how long she would have to pretend to be in a perfect marriage to a man who didn't want her.

"Lola! I didn't know you were here. Why aren't you sitting with us?"

It took Bianca a full three pulse beats to recognize that the sudden silence meant the remark had been directed at her. She turned from painting fresh lipstick on her mouth and watched a confused double take mar the other woman's flawless features.

As their befuddled silence stretched out, their spectators quit bothering to pretend they were washing hands or teasing their hair. They outright stared.

Betray nothing. Bianca was putting together that Lola might be short for Lolita, the name of the half sister she had never met. As her heart began to thud like running boots, she ruthlessly sculpted a bemused smile onto her face. She could feel the strain in her neck. Tension pulled her navel all the way into her spine. A cold sweat, sticky as tree sap, rose on her skin.

"I think you have me confused with someone else," Bianca managed to say.

"I do." The woman was frozen as she cataloged Bianca's face and hair and build. "I thought you were my brother's girlfriend. You look just like her."

Bianca tried to decide if it would do more damage than good to say something about how she was mistakenly recognized a lot lately. After seeing her on the news, people were constantly asking where they knew her from.

"My date is an only child," Bianca joked. "I don't think he's your brother."

The woman gave a little laugh, but it was more skeptical than amused. "Let's take a selfie. I'll send it to my brother. But first…" She placed a hand on her pregnant belly and pointed toward the stalls. "I'll be right out."

"Of course."

Talk about rude, Bianca was far worse than Everett. The moment the woman's back was turned, she bolted from the room, certain several pairs of eyebrows went up as she did. She kept her head down as she hurried back to Everett.

"I was hoping you'd be here," Roman Killian, TecSec's founder, shook the hand Everett extended. "I wasn't sure if you would thank me or fire me for sending that video to Giovanni."

"I wasn't in a fit state to clean up my own mess. I appreciate your involving him." Everett asked after Roman's family, learning everyone was thriving.

"And *your* wife?" Roman asked without a hint of facetiousness.

"Bianca's here with me." Everett shifted so he could watch for her and tried to shake off the tension that had taken hold as they had arrived here. He didn't like discord between them, and he especially didn't like her disappearing from sight when there was. "She's in the queue for the powder room, I imagine."

Like him, Roman preferred to converse side by side so he could keep an eye on the room. "She handled herself well in that emergency."

It was an innocuous comment, but the hair on the back of Everett's neck stood up. The back of Everett's throat dried and he wet it with champagne that now tasted sour.

"Why do you find that remarkable?"

Roman sent Everett a side-eye. "I may be overstepping again."

"Step," Everett commanded.

"Given that she nearly killed my client, I took it upon myself to run her name. At the time I only had the alias she had given your housekeeper."

"I ran Sandy Ortiz myself. There were several in New York, only a handful in her age group. No red flags. Her mother was clean, too."

"Which name did you use for her mother?"

"Isabel Palm—" Everett cut himself off. Swore. "She was Ortiz? Are you telling me that's Bianca's birth name?"

"I'm telling you that Isabel Ortiz gave birth to Alejandra Ortiz in New York on Bianca's birthday and the final instalment on her maternity bill was paid by Isabel Palmer a year later."

"Alejandra." Shortened to Sandy? His mind raced to find the implications, but so what if her mother had changed their names. That didn't mean Bianca was guilty of anything except hanging on to a piece of her family history. "Bianca doesn't know her father. Maybe her mother was hiding from him?"

"That's a good bet since there's an Alejandro Rodriguez in the Cuban Mafia here. They call him Sandro. Twenty-six years ago, he was heading into eight years for drug trafficking. His girlfriend, Isabel Ortiz, disappeared during court proceedings, but there was no follow-up, no missing person. Nothing from her family to raise an alarm."

Because Bianca's grandmother had known her daughter had gone to New York?

But if Bianca's mother had named her daughter after her lover, that suggested warmer feelings toward the man than fear or hatred.

"Where is Sandro now?" Everett asked, prickling with suspicion.

"Here. He had his rival killed while he was still inside. Allegedly," Roman added dryly. "He got out in five and played the game smarter after that. On the face of it, he makes his money with convenience stores, nightclubs and ATM machines that specialize in crypto."

All well-known means of laundering illicit funds. Everett swore again.

"Even if Bianca has that sort of connection, she doesn't seem to be using it," Everett noted. "She's been staying in my house, not his." Unless she's been in contact with her father all this time. Unless she knew who Everett was, who he used to be, and was gathering as much information as she could on him.

The things he had confided in her began to churn like broken glass in his belly.

"Here she comes." Roman arranged his face into welcoming interest.

Everett couldn't manage anything beyond the poker face he adopted when stakes went through the roof and his world was avalanching toward a pile of rubble.

Bianca didn't notice. She kept her head down and grasped his arm, nails digging through his sleeve with urgency.

"Can we go? I don't feel well," she blurted.

Despite the gaping valley of distrust that had opened between them, his heart swerved with alarm. He reflexively took hold of her elbow and shot a glower back the way she'd come.

"What happened?"

"I don't feel well. *Please?* I'm so sorry." She barely glanced at Roman. "I just really... Please? Right now?"

Everett offered the briefest of nods to Roman and escorted her through the crowd to fetch her wrap from the coat check. He waited until the privacy screen had enclosed them in the back of the car to ask again, "What happened?"

Everett's voice was surprisingly sharp. They'd been slightly at odds since entering that party, given their conflicted exchange on the way there. His shuttered expression had hardened even more, though. There was a piercing quality in his gaze that seemed to already know answers to questions he hadn't yet asked, making her want to squirm at hiding anything from him.

She couldn't tell him she had been in the same room as someone who knew her sibling, though.

She had never told anyone who her father was. Her mother had drilled into her that it was *their* secret. Bianca couldn't tell *anyone*. Ever.

"I told you, I don't feel well. I didn't mean to make a scene." Her insides were sloshing like a washing machine and there was a metallic taste under her tongue.

"Bianca—" he started to growl in warning.

"*No.*" She wagged a finger at him, tension igniting into temper. "You've been railroading my life since we *met*. I was going to do this whole thing on my own. You keep trying to make me feel guilty for dragging you into this, but *you* seduced *me*. *You* brought me into your house. *You* made me rely on you and you pretend you have my best interest at heart, but you *don't*. You're just using me for sex games and arm candy at your stupid parties! Why do I even have to do this?"

She could hear the hysteria climbing in her voice, but it was a cumulation of all she'd been through—abandoning her life, months and months of solitary confinement before being thrust into the limelight. *Him*. Taking over her thoughts and body and autonomy.

And now this. Putting her in danger of being discovered by the man her mother had gone to such pains to keep her hidden from.

"If being seen at parties was your main goal in life, you wouldn't be so bored out of your mind once you got there, so why are we going?" she charged. "Because I *hate* it. Quit making me go to these things. I don't want to meet a bunch of strangers for no reason. What do I even get out of it?"

His head had gone back as though buffeted by a strong wind.

"That's why you're upset? Because we went to a party and spoke to a few strangers? Did someone say something?"

"*Everyone* says something. I hate being on display like this." She was shaking, still freaking out at what a close brush she'd had. "Why did you even become involved with me? You're making my life worse, you know. I did the right thing." She jabbed at her chest. "I pointed out a crime. Why do I have to be questioned for hours and wear clothes that aren't even comfortable and get noticed wherever I go? Why do I have to have *my* life destroyed so you can keep yours?"

She clamped her mouth tight and sniffed back gathering tears, looking to the window as she tried to hold herself together. She never should have stayed in Miami. That was the problem. Nearly being recognized by someone who knew her father was her fault, not Everett's.

But there was a piece of her still standing in that powder room, wanting to beg, *Tell me more. What are they like? Take me to them.*

She heard the rustle of Everett's jacket and

the subtle beep of him placing a call. "Bianca needs a break."

She jerked her head around. "Who is that?"

"What do you mean you 'can't dictate these things'?" Everett asked in a deadly tone. "Anything you can't do can be done by a better lawyer. Shall I find one? Because Ackerley's people are dragging this out to exhaust her, hoping she'll stumble. Quit playing into their hands."

"Is that my lawyer?" Bianca hissed. "Don't fire him!" She liked him.

"Cancel all of them," Everett said. "Tell them she'll be in New York at the end of the month. They can have one more meeting when we get there. Beyond that, they can wait until they're in court." He ended the call.

"By all means, keep taking over my life," she said scathingly. "Does it occur to you that I might prefer to get this over with?"

"It will take years before this is over. Perhaps never," he said bluntly.

She knew that. Deep inside, she had known that from the moment she had realized what was going on at Morris and Ackerley and that she was the only person who could stop it. She had known her actions would cause her to lose her job, her home, her friendships. Even most of her freedom.

It was still hard to accept. The fact that Everett was so pitiless about it made it a thousand times worse.

"It's my experience, Bianca, that when someone *appears*—I use that word deliberately." He tucked his phone away. "I'm not saying you're overreacting, but when someone *appears* to be overreacting— Quit prickling up."

She sat so straight all her hair was nearly on end. "You mean quit overreacting?"

"When someone *appears* to be reacting more strongly than a situation warrants," he continued in a firm tone. "For instance, when they run out of a building as though it's on fire and it's not, it means they have been pushed to their limit by factors I can't see. In your case, the ones that I *can* see are the long days of making statements and the long evenings talking to strangers who put you on the spot. By removing those pressures, I'm freeing you up to react however you must to some of the others."

His hand moved restlessly on his thigh before he added, "I didn't realize you felt used by our lovemaking."

"Don't call it *lovemaking* when you have no intention of loving me," she spat. Then she wanted to cringe into a ball of humiliation. Her throat was squeezed so tight, she could barely swallow, let alone talk. "I wish I could compartmentalize like you do, but I can't."

"So that's what this is really about? Our talk

earlier? You're angry that I told you why we don't have a future?"

"I'm angry that you keep trying to shape my future when you don't even want to be a part of it."

Bianca went to bed as soon as they arrived home.

Everett poured himself a Scotch, then brought up his copy of tonight's guest list and examined it again.

She was angry at him and the things they'd discussed on the way to the party. He accepted that. But that wasn't the only reason she was upset. She had been withdrawn at the party until she'd gone to the powder room. Now that he knew she had more than a nascent connection to her father—she had been given a version of the man's first name, for instance—he had to wonder if she'd met with someone who had spooked her.

He had reviewed this guest list prior to their leaving the house. If he had seen anyone on there that concerned him, he wouldn't have taken her there in the first place. He still couldn't see who might have upset her so badly she would insist on cutting their evening short, then lose her temper with him.

He texted Roman and asked him to run the guest list through his database to identify known associates. The resources Everett had access to were good and he had the skills to fill in blanks manually, but that took time. TecSec scraped social media and other ancillary connections with the push of a button.

While he waited, he mentally reviewed all that Bianca had said, searching for clues between the lines. A lot of air came out of a distressed tire, but not all of it. He addressed each of her indictments in turn, starting with the one that had kicked him in the teeth.

You're using me for sex games and arm candy.

He was using the *events*, not her, but it was true, she benefited very little from their appearances. Those pantomimes were PR events, and she was right. He mostly loathed them, but he'd been enjoying them more lately, mostly because when they were out like that, he could let others ask her questions and watch her smile and grow animated. God knew he stood taller having such a gorgeous woman beside him. He could hold her hand and smell her hair and react purely the way he wanted to without giving up anything of himself.

You keep trying to make me feel guilty for dragging you into this, but you seduced me.

He had. Against his better judgment, in fact.

I'm angry that you keep trying to shape my future when you don't even want to be a part of it.

202 CINDERELLA FOR THE MIAMI PLAYBOY

That wasn't quite true. He was already dreading when this would be over, and they would have to say goodbye.

Don't call it lovemaking *when you have no intention of loving me.*

He rubbed the heel of his hand against his breastbone, unable to erase the burning ache behind it. His inhale and exhale scalded his lungs.

Thankfully, his phone pinged with the notification of a shared file from Roman, dragging him from a pool of rumination that was deeper than he was prepared to dive into.

He replied.

Thanks.

NP. I'm always looking for people with your skill set, FYI.

Everett snorted. He would get right on that, seeing as it had been working out so well for him lately.

He opened the file and clicked through it, searching for anyone with the last name of Rodriguez. Given the demographics in this city, it was no surprise he came across a dozen. Even more had associations to people with that same last name, but he soon drilled down to one guest who had a brother dating one Lolita Rodriguez, daughter of Sandro.

A quick flick to Lolita's social feed revealed her to be in her early twenties and a dead ringer for Bianca. Everett's brain exploded.

This was *exactly* what had happened to Giovanni. He'd let his fly do his thinking and missed some life-threatening details.

Swearing under his breath, Everett snatched up his phone to make a call. They were going off-grid and let's see Bianca dance away from his questions when she had nowhere left to go.

CHAPTER NINE

"Is this the yacht you were coming to inspect when we met?" Bianca asked as Everett piloted the tender toward the stern of the *Abeona*.

The two-hundred-foot craft was named for the goddess of outward journeys, he had told her when he asked her to pack for a week.

She had agreed because it had seemed like a small peace offering and, after nearly being recognized last night, she was anxious to get out of Miami. A trip down the Keys would give her a little breathing room to figure out her next steps.

She never should have stayed in Florida. It was one thing when all her online photos had been dated corporate headshots, but now that she was constantly being photographed with Everett, something like last night had become inevitable.

"It is," he replied, maintaining the circumspect tone he'd been using all morning. He was being his inscrutable self, unfailingly polite and effortlessly sexy in his casual control as he lowered the boat from its top speed to smoothly guide it into place.

She bit back a sigh. She'd had plenty of time to regret her outburst while she'd been lying in bed alone all night. She was still distraught, but now it mostly centered around how embarrassed she was that she'd brought up the *L*-word. She wished she hadn't revealed how much his detachment bothered her. He might have set the rules, but she had agreed to them. She had no right to complain.

"I guess I wouldn't have missed your arrival if you had pulled up in this," she joked, hoping to soften him a little, but he only cut the motor and moved swiftly to throw the line to a waiting crewman on the yacht.

Moments later, Everett helped her step onto the lower deck of the yacht where he introduced her to Captain Garcia, then the first mate and steward, Raj and Sheila.

Everett nodded for the yacht to get underway as soon as the tender was secured before offering Bianca a tour.

"It's a lean crew at the moment, since it's only us aboard," Everett informed her. "Crew quarters are on this deck and there are four staterooms for guests. We'll go up to the main deck here."

They took the stairs on the starboard side of the stern and arrived on a lido deck. Here the sparkle from the blue of the pool reflected off the underside of the blue-and-white awning that shaded nearby lounge chairs.

Bianca couldn't help gasp as they walked into the main saloon, which was all curved lines and gleaming chrome. Comfortable sectionals with silk tasseled pillows gave way to a glass-topped oval dining table that sat ten. A horseshoe-shaped bar was stationed beneath a tryptic of abstract paintings. That art seemed to be the inspiration for the color scheme of ivory and silver-blue with accents of deep navy and frosty greens.

She would have thought herself in a top floor penthouse in New York if not for the windows that offered unobstructed views of the Florida coastline and the open Atlantic.

"This is beautiful. No wonder you had to have it."

He started to say something but seemed to think better of it.

"What?" she prompted.

"Aside from my small obsession with cars, I'm not particularly attached to any of my properties, but I bought it after I'd met you and wondered what you would think of it."

She was momentarily befuddled by what sounded like an admission that she had held some importance in his decision. Maybe he wanted to smooth over things, too.

"I think it's beautiful, obviously."

He waved for her to move around the partition wall behind the bar, where a foyer accessed both the port and starboard decks.

On the wall between them, a pair of double doors stood open, allowing them to enter the master stateroom. It was also styled with chrome and curves and sumptuous comfort. Her gaze was drawn first to the skylight over the massive bed, then the desk on one side and S-shaped sofa on the other. A private deck with glass railings invited her to walk out to the bow. She sighed with reflexive bliss as she took in rippled water and endless sky and swooping gulls.

Everett joined her and set his hands on the edge of the Plexiglas rail.

"Last night, you accused me of trying to make you feel guilty for dragging me into your controversy."

"I shouldn't have agreed to dinner in the first place. I should have realized—"

"No." He held up a hand. "You were right. I knew something was up but pursued you anyway."

She was so relieved that they were clearing the air, all her defenses crumbled away. "I still could have been more honest."

"Yes. You could have," he said gravely. He turned his head, and his gaze was so impactful she grasped at the rail, feeling off-balance.

It's a boat, she reminded herself, and glanced around to catch her bearings. The breeze was picking up, rippling his shirt and the hem of her sundress. They had begun to move. That's why she felt off-kilter.

But his words had thrown her. She immediately felt pushed onto the defensive and now saw he was as composed and unassailable as always. She had thought they were both giving a little, but no. Only her. He was fully in command.

"I understand why you didn't tell me about the whistleblowing when we were only meant to be ships passing in the night," he continued in that voice that was ever so neutral. Why did that hurt more than if he had been angry and hard? "But you've had nearly two weeks to tell me the rest, Bianca."

"There is no 'rest,'" she insisted, but she couldn't hold his gaze.

She instinctually glanced at the narrow stairs behind him. They seemed to lead to an upper deck, but she decided against trying to brush past him and went back into the suite. She came up short as she realized he had closed the doors to the foyer when they had come in. Where did she even think she could run to? They were on a freaking boat, dry land growing smaller at a rapid pace.

She snapped a look at him as he came in behind her.

"I was only keeping Sheila from interrupting us. Leave the room if you want to, but this conversation will happen. We're staying aboard until it does. Alejandra."

Her knees nearly buckled, and her throat strangled on whatever words she was trying to form. Her muscles all began to twitch, the urge to fight or flee making her heart pound like a sledgehammer in her chest.

"That's just a name I used…"

"Don't embarrass yourself," he said in that voice so devoid of emotion. He leaned on the rounded corner of a wall. "I know that Sandy Ortiz is your birth name. I know who your father is. I know who you met last night. I want to know what was said that had you running out of there so fast. A threat? What have you told Sandro Rodriguez since you came to Miami? What have you told him since you moved into my *house*?"

Bianca threw her head back, astounded. And guilty. Yes. But how had he learned all of that? Did it mean others knew as well? The adrenaline in her system intensified and, because she felt so cornered, she went on the attack.

"So this isn't you trying to give me a break or patch things up between us. You brought me onto a floating cell for further interrogation. I hate your yacht, Everett. I think it's a giant piece of litter owned by a lying, opportunist of a man. Go soak your head." She started toward the door, but what was she going to do? Jump overboard and ride a dolphin to shore?

"I didn't hear a denial."

She spun around and came back. She was shaking so hard it frightened her, but she was both scared and mad. Scared that her secret, the one she had protected so carefully all these years, had been discovered and furious that he was throwing it out at her as though she had any choice in the matter.

"I told you I've never met my father. That's true. Yes, Sandro Rodriguez conceived me with my mother, but he doesn't know I exist. My mother never told him she was pregnant. She didn't even say goodbye to him."

It felt strange to speak of it, as though she was toppling something sacred. Her mother could have taken the identity of Bianca's father to her grave. Instead, she had answered all of Bianca's questions, then had sworn her to secrecy.

Telling Everett was like breaking that last bond Bianca had shared with her mother. It made her feel as though she was betraying her. It hurt and felt wrong, and she was ashamed of herself for crumbling so easily, but once the first trickle of truth spilled out, the rest swelled up, insisting on gushing forth.

"She realized she was pregnant while he was waiting to be sentenced. By then, people were trying to kill him. He couldn't protect her from behind bars, so Mom moved to New York and changed our name as soon as she was able to."

"Did she testify against him? Was she afraid of him?"

"She was *in love* with him." She hugged herself, cold despite the humid tropical air drifting in from the open doors to the bow. "They were planning to marry, but they kept it a secret because my grandmother didn't approve of him."

"Because he was a criminal?"

"Because he was *poor*," she said tersely. "And because it genuinely went against my grandmother's beliefs for Mom to have sex out of wedlock. She and my father were both very young and he wound up making some terrible choices trying to prove he could give Mom a good life. He was angry when he realized Mom had left. He called my grandmother and lost his temper. She wouldn't have anything to do with Mom after that because *she* was afraid of him."

That had weighed heavily on her mother. Bianca had seen it.

"And you?"

"Me? Oh, you care about me now?" Her throat was so thick she could hardly speak.

She resented that flinty look of his. It was exactly in line with all the questioning she'd undergone this week and told her exactly how little she or her situation was impacting him. He was turning her inside out while remaining detached as a lover, a friend, or even a pretend husband.

"By the time I was old enough to beg Mom to tell me about him, he was out of prison, married and staring his new family. Mom impressed on me that there would be no getting that cat back in the bag if I reached out to him, and there would be a lot of consequences if I did. I had to be very sure if I ever decided to take the step of trying to meet him. That's why I was upset last night." She paced a few restless steps, rubbing her bare arms. "A woman mistook me for m-my—" She cleared her throat. "My half sister."

"Lolita."

"Yes." The name scored across her heart deep enough to make her flinch. She had snooped on the young woman's social feeds in the past. It was like looking at her college self with a deeper tan and more fashion sense. There was a familiarity to her half brothers' features that made her wistful, too.

"If you're so afraid of running into them, why stay in Miami? Why use your *birth* name?"

"It's not exactly unique here," she scoffed, then swallowed, trying to ease the constriction that was causing her voice to quaver, but a corkscrew was lodged in her chest, turning and turning. "They're the only family I have. I had to walk away from every other part of my life, but that part still felt…possible."

His eyes narrowed. "So you *do* want to meet them."

"Of course, I want to meet them!" she cried, waving a helpless hand. "I always have, but I *can't*. I don't know how they would react. I don't want to destroy his marriage or ruin his relationship with his children. I can't imagine he'll want anything to do with me now I'm a whistleblower," she said with a broken, humorless laugh. "He would be suspicious as hell, and I wouldn't blame him. More importantly, who knows what his enemies would do if they found out he has another child? That's why Mom made me take a blood oath never to tell anyone. Not a best friend. Not a boss or a boyfriend or a *husband*."

His mouth tightened, telling her the sarcasm stung, but it wasn't the least bit satisfying. She was starting to cry, and it just made her more furious. She smacked at her cheeks to whisk the tears away.

"It's always been this huge, impossible balloon that sits inside me, making it hard to breathe. Sometimes it gets so big, I think it will burst and kill me. Other times, I think she was right to hide me from him. As long as we were the only ones who knew who I am, that part of his life couldn't hurt me."

"I'm the only one who knows," he said firmly, adding begrudgingly, "And Roman Killian, but he makes his living keeping secrets. It won't go any further than that."

"And we'll just assume that woman last night won't mention it to *anyone*? She wanted a selfie so she could text her brother." Bianca had been trying not to dwell on what might have happened after she left but given the fact her face was plastered everywhere these days, she thought the odds were good that her father would become aware of her and start to wonder. Others might, too.

"Just…" She sniffed and grabbed up a few tissues to blow her nose. "Let me off somewhere so I can…get lost."

His head went back as if she'd delivered an upper cut. The rest of his body stayed so still he seemed to be made of marble.

"I'm not dropping you on some island to fend for yourself," he stated grimly.

"Why not? You said this cruise would last until we had this conversation. It happened. Now take me back to shore." Her whole body was condensing with so much tension, she felt made of iron. Cold and hard and heavy and black all the way to her soul. If he dropped her overboard, she would sink straight to the bottom like an anchor.

"I need to make some calls." He pushed off the wall.

"We had an agreement!"

"Where would you go, Bianca? Hmm?" he challenged with impatience. "You know what's out there waiting for you. Now so do I. So no. You're not leaving this yacht. Not until I've arranged all those protections I promised you."

"I don't want you to keep paying for my problems!" She nearly stamped her foot like a child.

"It is my problem! Who took you to that party? I did," he snapped, thumbing into his chest. "I knew something wasn't right, but I put it down to our tiff in the car."

"Oh, my God, Everett." She choked on a laugh, genuinely astonished that she was coming to his defense when she was furious with him, but, "You can't actually predict every bad thing that might happen. You know that, don't you?"

He pinched the bridge of his nose, swearing. "It's the same damned feeling I had when I let Giovanni head straight into that ambush. I should have known."

"It's not the same," she cried, but there was a knock at the door, and he brushed past her to open it.

"Sheila. Go ahead and unpack Bianca. I'll sleep in another room." He took his bag from the startled steward and disappeared.

CHAPTER TEN

EVERETT FOUND BIANCA an hour later. She was reading in the shade next to the pool, wearing a bikini with a strapless top in neon yellow and tiny striped bottoms in yellow and lime green.

He swallowed and averted his gaze to the horizon as he lowered himself to sit sideways on the lounger next to hers. A glint on the water pierced into his brain.

"Do you ever sunbathe topless?" he asked abruptly.

"Dream on!" She glanced down at her top and that jerked his attention to where her nipples betrayingly poked against the cups.

Their gazes collided and her cheeks flushed.

"I'm advising you don't." He nodded at a flash of light. "Long lens camera."

"Ugh." For a moment, she looked like she would weep at yet another invasion of her privacy.

"Would you rather talk inside?"

"I'd rather read my book in peace," she mut-

tered, closing it in her lap. "The king of a ficti-
tious Mediterranean island had just kidnapped
the heroine onto his yacht." She batted her lashes
while her mouth wore a curl of irony. "Life imi-
tates art yet again."

Don't, he ordered himself, but his body immediately conjured the sensation of her hands
smearing suntan oil all over his body. He imagined working the fragrant oil into her smooth
skin and flexing muscles before sliding their
slippery bodies together as the afternoon sun
burnished their skin to gold.

He took a gulp of the slushy drink on the table
between their chairs, trapped ever deeper inside
a medieval torture device, one that impaled him
in a thousand places, making every movement
and breath its own world of agony.

He had done this. He had seduced her against
his better judgment and started all these domi-
noes falling. But…

"I stand by my decision to help you." He set
down the sweating glass and dried his hand on
the leg of his shorts. "Even if you'd managed
to evade being tracked down, Ackerley was already destroying your credibility. The wheels
of justice turn very slowly, and you would have
been ground to bits in its gears long before it
gets where it's going. I'll make no apology for
providing you a fortress to hide in along with a
team to represent you. I've ordered you a dedi-

cated security detail and I have an agent finding you an apartment in New York—"

"I have an apartment in New York," she cut in.

"You *had* a sublet bedroom in a building that doesn't even have a doorman, let alone a proper alarm system."

"You can't keep buying me things, Everett."

"I can and I will. It'll take a week or so, but everything will be in place by the time we get back to Miami. I'll take you to New York myself then…" A searing pain bloomed in his chest. "Then I'll distance myself so I'm not drawing that extra attention onto you."

"And issue a statement that we're taking a break?" Her voice cracked and she turned her face away.

She must have immediately realized the camera was catching whatever emotions were on her face because she made a frustrated noise and abruptly rose. A moment later, she threw herself into a cushioned corner behind him.

He rubbed his hands together, fleetingly thinking of Lady Macbeth failing to clean the stains from her hands. "It's for the best, Bianca."

"You don't know what's best for me," she snapped.

"I know what is *not* best for you." He rose so he could turn and face her. "Me."

"Is that your clairvoyant superpower telling

you that? Did the government know you were bitten by a radioactive spider? Is that why they hired you?"

"They hired me because I am a dog with a bone. I don't quit until I've gnawed it clean, even if it means I'm surrounded by wolves who want to fight me for it. They hired me because I *like* being in that fight. Believe me when I tell you that you don't want to be with a man who is willing to risk everything for the high of proving he can come out on top. That's why we're in this mess right now."

"You really do think you're above the flaw of being human, don't you? You screwed up, Everett. We all do it, despite our best intentions. I did." She waved at herself, voice scraped raw. "I went ahead and fell in love with you, even though I swore to myself I wouldn't."

"Don't—" He held up a hand as if it could stop that bullet from piercing his chest, but bittersweet agony blossomed through his body anyway. "Why the hell would you do that? Now I'm going to hurt you even more."

"When?"

"What?" He dropped his hand.

"When are you going to hurt me? In a week, when you leave me in New York? Or while we're on this yacht? Because I will not let you spend a week turning the knife just so you can prove what a lousy man you are to love."

He flexed his hands, biting out, "Stop saying that."

"That I love you? Why? Does it hurt?"

"Yes."

Her shoulders sagged with defeat and her brow pleated. "It's supposed to be a good thing, Everett. It's supposed to make you feel like you matter."

He looked away, aching from his scalp to his toes. *Don't say it.* He clenched his teeth, but had to say, "You matter. Okay, Bianca? You matter to me. That's why— *Oof."*

Her body crashed into his and he reflexively caught her close as he staggered to keep his balance.

Then the reality, the *joy* of holding her, exploded within him. He told himself to let her go, but he couldn't. The best he could do was close his eyes and tuck her face into his neck while he smoothed his hand over her silky hair. She was shaking and so was he, both of them far more affected by their conversation than they were letting on.

"I am human. I do know that," he told her. "I don't have any superpower where you're concerned. It's more of a fatal weakness. That's why I'm trying to protect you. If you really understood who I am—"

"Show me," she insisted, tilting back her head to stare straight into his eyes. "I want that man.

Not a tycoon or a spy or… I just want you. The *real* you."

Did she? Because that man snapped free of what constraints he had left. He released her, but only to stoop and throw her over his shoulder. He started to the master stateroom.

Bianca's breath left her in a squeal of shock. She grabbed handfuls of his shirt as Everett carried her through the saloon where one of the crew gave a cough of surprised laughter, then mumbled a daunted apology.

She didn't see who it was. Her hair was in her eyes and, as Everett entered the stateroom and pivoted to close and lock the doors, she threw an arm over her head in protection.

"I'm not going to let you bump your head," he muttered, sounding insulted. He swung her into the cradle of his arms before lightly dropping her onto the bed.

She caught fistfuls of the covers as she found her bearings again.

"So we're doing Tarzan and Jane?" she asked as he closed the doors to the bow and dropped the blinds.

"We're doing Everett and Bianca. This is who I am. I'm not as civilized as I pretend, Bianca. Now I want to see *you*." He came to the edge of the bed and caught her by the ankle, dragging her closer so he could twist his hand in her bikini bottoms and start to peel them off.

She gasped and thrust her hand down to cover her mound.

He froze. "No?"

"This feels really..."

"Frightening?" His hold on her bottoms loosened, and he drew back slightly, banking the lust that gleamed in his eyes.

"Intimate," she said. "Like we've never done it before." Like they couldn't come back from it. "I'm nervous."

The stern look eased from his face, and he flowed onto the bed, covering her and pressing her into the mattress, caging her as he propped himself on his elbows over her.

"But you know I'd never force you or hurt you. You trust me." It wasn't a question. He knew she did. Deep in his eyes, navy blue flecks gleamed like reverse stars in the sky blue of his irises, mingling with clouds of lust and possessiveness and something so tender, she began to shake inside.

She slid her hands from his chest around his rib cage to the indent of his spine. "I do."

She loved him. But she didn't say it. She showed him. She curled her legs around his waist and touched between his shoulder blades and relaxed beneath him, lifting her mouth to invite his kiss.

He swooped his mouth onto hers, hotly claiming. She welcomed the rake of his hungry lips, reveling in his ravishment. His whole weight pinned her a moment as he flattened himself on her, briefly dominating her before he pulled himself back under control with a hiss.

As he gathered his weight onto his knee and elbow, and tucked his tormented brow into her neck, she said, "Don't hold back, Everett. I want all of you. I can take it."

With a feral noise, he opened his mouth on her neck in damp suction, then licked up the throbbing artery to her mouth again. His kiss nearly smothered her before turning to something that tasted of agony and need and sweet, sweet veneration.

He slid down to kiss across her collarbone, over the swells of her breasts, then dragged the bikini top down to expose her nipple. When the hot cavern of his mouth enclosed the turgid tip, she groaned and slid her fingers into his hair.

He lifted his head and showed his teeth in cruel enjoyment.

"I like hearing that," he said grittily, dragging her hands from his hair and pinning her wrists in one hand above her head. "When you make those noises, I know you're feeling exactly the way I am, like you're going to die from the want." He licked at her nipple, blew softly. "Now come for me."

He began to suckle at her, drawing on one breast then the other, making her writhe beneath him. Hot runnels of desire flooded into her loins, again and again. She made all the noises for him, growing so aroused she was going mad with it.

"Everett, I can't. I can't," she cried, nearly weeping with sexual frustration.

"No?" He brought his head up to suck on her bottom lip, still palming one of her breasts. "You're so close, but I don't want to bruise you. Tell me what you need." His hand trailed down to rub her bare abdomen, circling and circling.

She didn't know why that made her pant, but it did. Delicious tingles shot from her nape into her nipples, from behind her navel into her sex.

"You." She turned her wrists with protest in his grip. "Let me touch you. Let me feel you inside me."

He reared up on his knees and threw off his shirt, then yanked down the fly of his shorts. As he drew them off and threw them away, she peeled her bikini off. He tossed it off the bed once her feet were free and stayed on his knees above her, fiercely sexual with his bronze tan and sculpted muscles and erection thrusting blatantly from the nest of hair at the crux of his powerful thighs.

Propped on her elbow, she took him in her fist, compelled to hold and caress and shift to take him in her mouth. She was helpless before him, before *this*. She really was. That knowledge had been terrifying right from the beginning and would worry her now if she wasn't drowning in stronger sensations of sharp excitement and greedy desire. In a need to *show* him that she was his. Utterly and completely. She fondled his backside and felt his firm globes flex. Saw his abdomen tighten as a groan rattled in his chest.

She might have smiled with cruel delight then, but he cupped her cheek and pulled away.

He muttered something about trying to last and swept his thumb across her wet lips, hand shaking. "I want to do that to you, but I can't wait."

She dropped onto her back and bent her knees, opening her legs in invitation.

With a groan, he swept his hand down her body and combed his fingers into the tangle of wet curls. Another, deeper groan left him as his fingers drew patterns in the abundant moisture, making her arch and moan.

"Everett, *please*." She started to close her fist on him again, but with a tortured growl, he stretched himself across the bed and dipped into the night table.

A hard jolt went through her. She hadn't given a thought to protection, but of course he had.

That was good, she reminded herself. He

didn't want children and she wouldn't force him to have any, but a poignant ache opened inside her when he swooped to cover her again.

His mouth sealed to hers as his hips pressed. His broad shape invaded. When his muscled thighs were hard where they held hers open, and the fine hairs on his legs scraped her inner thighs, she bent her knees and drew her ankles to his hips, tilting her hips to invite him deeper. He gathered her beneath him and let his weight settle heavily on her pelvis, ensuring they were as indelibly connected as they could possibly be.

I love you, she thought as she shaped his skull and caressed his neck and stroked over his bunched shoulders. She brushed light kisses across his mouth and jaw and cheekbone. If she couldn't have forever with him, she would remember every tiny detail of this moment when his spicy scent was making her drunk.

His eyes closed for the press of her mouth on his eyelid and a growl of pleasure reverberated in his chest. Inside her, he was hot and pulsing and his first shallow thrust made the world glitter.

"Look at me," he lifted his head to rasp.

She did, barely able to withstand the intimacy of their locked stare. This was raw and primal, and all her shields were gone. There was no hiding anything from him. Not now. Especially not her heart. It was there, offered freely, if only he would accept it.

His brow flexed in anguish, but he didn't hide from the light in her gaze. He studied her face as though memorizing it. His hand cradled her jaw and he kissed her softly, then with more heat, as though he couldn't help himself.

A small tension gathered in him, and he clasped her tight as he rolled them.

Startled to find herself on top, she adjusted her knees and arched with pleasure as his palms swept over her back and hips and buttocks.

"Better," he said with a tone of agreement. "Now take everything you need from me."

There was a pinch inside her heart. He must know what she wanted most from him, but as he gathered each of her breasts in his wide palms, fairly worshipping them in the way he gently cradled and brushed his thumbs against her nipples, and his gaze continued to stray over her as though she was the most glorious thing he'd ever seen, she thought maybe he was giving her everything he was capable of giving.

Her whole body throbbed with need. She wanted nothing more than for him to thrust with all his power, imprinting himself on her and taking her over the edge into ecstasy. But she leaned into that touch, lost to the bliss of it for a few breathless moments.

Then she let her hands roam over his muscled

chest, luxuriating in the meatiness of his pecs, the ripples of his rib cage and the light line of hair down his abdomen. She did everything she could to pleasure both of them, stroking over his skin and licking at his nipples, making his chest swell and his breath hiss audibly.

She touched herself as she began to move on him. She rode him and watched through slitted eyes as his cheeks darkened and his lips drew into a grimace of tension. He made a noise of gratification, and his hands came to her hips, guiding her as he thrust up to meet her.

When he was a hard line beneath her and she was in danger of tipping over the edge into the abyss, she slowed and drew out each lift and return of her hips. She folded onto him so she could kiss him as she lived in the eternity of taking him to the edge of leaving her, then sinking back into the return so they both exhaled in relief.

His heart was hammering against her breast. His teeth caught at her lip. Her nipples scraped the hair on his chest and her insides quivered with tension. He was shaking beneath her, and she was trembling atop him. His breath was uneven as he fought to maintain control.

"I won't break until you do," she told him.

"Damn it, Bianca. Damn you." He wrapped his arms around her and thrust up, releasing ragged groans as he shuddered, and his erection pulsed hotly inside her.

She had no room in her for smugness. As his hips lifted hers off the bed, the sun exploded, and she was lost in the white-hot light of her own ecstasy.

She had completely unraveled him and continued to do so over the ensuing days. It was disturbing, opening places in Everett that had closed over like scar tissue, aching, but thick and protected. Now there was a sensation that was fresh and exposed, sensitive to each look from her. Each smile. Each kiss and caress.

He wasn't sure how he'd convinced himself he could make love to her and not feel her love as a gentle, persistent breeze that wore down all his hard edges. He hadn't, of course. He had been sure she would break off those pieces and leave him as a pile of moraine, but he hadn't cared. He was opportunistic enough to steal this time with her while he could. The later costs were negligible against the precious value these memories would hold for him.

He stored every moment in his mental vault as they made love and talked and swam and fished and strapped on tanks for scuba diving. It was like an enchantment to float in that blue, silent, timeless world, where the colorful fish had nothing on the graceful movements of her golden body and the delight in her eyes when she looked at him from behind her mask. Later, they would sit around reading and eating and behaving with unabashed hedonism, touching and teasing until they rose to find the nearest bed and make love again.

But he knew this was a new game they were playing, a new lie they were telling themselves. They wanted to believe they had forever, but they only had today and maybe a little bit of tomorrow. They wouldn't know until they got there. They talked about everything except that.

The clock wound down when they returned to Key Largo. They were mellow after a lovemaking-induced nap, sipping wine as the sun set. Flames of ruby and marmalade danced around them, reflecting off chrome and glass.

"I hate to spoil a moment," Sheila murmured as she topped up their glasses, "But your lawyer asked me to convey that he would very much like you to return his call at your earliest convenience."

"I saw there were a couple of messages from him," Bianca confessed with a wrinkle of her nose at Everett. She was snuggled under his arm, her bent legs tucked warmly against his thigh. "Do you mind?"

He did, but, "He wouldn't ask you to interrupt his dinner if it wasn't important."

She placed the call and held the phone so Everett could listen.

"Morris and Ackerley have negotiated a settlement," her lawyer said. "They will pay a fine and abstain from similar business for five years in order to avoid further investigation. There won't be any court proceedings or further charges. Bianca still needs to testify to a congressional committee, but that won't happen for several months. It's over."

"Over," Bianca said with disbelief.

Over. Everett had known that train was coming, but he still hadn't anticipated how quickly it would arrive. Or how it would travel through him and leave such a massive cavity.

"Are you still coming to New York as scheduled? I can give you all the details then, but I wanted you to know."

"Thank you. Yes, we're sailing back to Miami overnight and will fly to New York in the morning." Everett took the phone from Bianca's limp fingers and ended the call.

"They should have been arrested," she said with helpless anger. "I went through all of this so they could buy their way out of it and start doing it again in a few years? That's not *fair.*"

"It's not." But if he had a penny for every injustice he'd failed to right despite his best efforts… Well, he pretty much did, and he was pretty damned wealthy.

Everett didn't let his churning emotions engulf him, though. He snapped his mind to the practicalities.

"My concern is retaliation. You'll still need that security detail. I would suggest a visit to Freja as soon as possible. Their compound is very secure and big enough you won't feel cooped up. I'll make arrangements so you can fly to Sicily the minute you've finished with your lawyer." He reached for his own phone.

"*Stop it*," Bianca cried, lurching to her feet so fast her stemless wineglass nearly toppled over.

He steadied it, then looked up at her, noting the misery gleaming in her eyes.

"Get it out then," he commanded.

"Don't you *dare* act as if this is a tantrum. I am not your pet project, Everett. I'm not your employee. I'm not even your *wife*. As evidenced by the fact you can't *wait* to get rid of me."

He clenched his teeth against saying, *That's not true*. But this breakup was necessary. A little hatred on her end would go a long way to making it quick and clean. To making it stick.

God, he could hardly bear to think of that.

"You're not even going to try to let me down easy?" Her throat flexed as she looked to the horizon. She was blinking fast, fighting not to reveal how badly he was hurting her, but he knew. He felt it inside him as a thousand turning knives.

"Look what I've done to you," he said with quiet anguish. "I've already caused you a lot of pain and it's been, what? Three weeks? You think that's going to change in another three weeks? In three years? If you give me the power to hurt you, I will. It's not even a risk. It's a given. Do you want that? I don't!"

"Neither do I," she said in a small, dignified voice.

Something in her tone caused a great hand to take hold of his chest, slowly closing into a fist, crushing his lungs into his heart until they were a ball of agony.

"But *love* is a risk," she said with a note of torment. "It hurts and terrifies and makes you feel worthless because how could you ever be as good as that other person wants you to be? Sometimes the people you love make mistakes and let you down and sometimes they even *die*. Love wrecks *everything*." She swept out a hand in emphasis. "But I'll tell you what, Everett. If you ever want to do something that makes you feel alive, genuinely alive and powerful and free, then fall in love." She stood tall and brushed the wetness off her cheek. "Until then, you go ahead and hide from it, so *you* don't get hurt. Thank you for your assistance. I can take it from here."

She walked away.

CHAPTER ELEVEN

BIANCA DIDN'T SLEEP a wink, nor did she shed a tear. Her devastation was too complete. She loved him and love was never wasted, but that would be her solace sometime in the future. For now, she could only lie still and suffer the pain while wondering when she had developed such a horrific taste for self-destruction.

While her mother had been alive, she'd been the ultimate good girl, earning straight As, rarely drinking, and never having sex on the first date. In the last year, she'd blown up her career, walked away from her life and had fallen in love with a man who refused to even try to make a future with her.

As if that wasn't the worst thing life could throw at her, when she rose in the early hours, she discovered she wasn't pregnant.

She didn't *want* to be pregnant, not really. Not if it would only trap Everett into sticking by her. She didn't want to lie to him about something like that either or exclude him from their child's life. He'd been super careful, so there hadn't really been a chance for her to conceive anyway. She hadn't had any genuine expectation that she would get pregnant, but as long as the possibility had been out there it had been that—a possibility. A tiny fantasy that could have sustained her a little longer.

But no. It was not to be and that felt like a death blow. They were definitely parting forever after this.

He appeared on deck when she did, having slept elsewhere. He must have slept at least a little because he didn't look nearly as much like dirty laundry as she felt. He was freshly shaved and wore a clean shirt and pressed trousers.

She didn't let herself take more than that snapshot of a glance, focusing on the travel mug of coffee Sheila handed her, but she felt Everett's gaze on her like a persistent hornet searching for a place to land.

"Your things from the house were packed and put in the vehicle that will pick us up from the marina," Everett said.

She didn't say anything, only sipped her coffee and watched Raj load their luggage from the yacht onto the tender.

Maybe she would speak to Everett once they were on the plane. That would have some symmetry. They could say their goodbyes in the air, the way they'd once said hello. She would tell him she was sorry she had called him a coward because who was she to accuse him of such a thing when she had never worked up the courage to meet her own father? Everett had done all sorts of brave, generous, forgiving things, including moving her into his house and paying for her upkeep, despite what she had eventually cost him.

Really, when she considered how much trouble she had been, was it any wonder he'd rather part ways as soon as possible?

Hide from it so you don't get hurt...

Good God, that woman knew how to throw out an insult, essentially calling him a coward, while also issuing a nearly irresistible dare.

Everett had been brooding all night, trying to logic his way out of the impossible position she'd put him in. He was trying to protect her, damn it, from himself. From his selfish impulses, the ones that were urging him to keep her and lock her into a lifetime of anguish.

Judging by how bruised her eyes looked, he'd already broken her heart. He hated himself for it, but if that was inevitable, surely letting her go now, so she could move on, was the kinder thing to do?

He averted his mind from thoughts of her with another man, of her making love and children with someone else. She'd be a really good mother, though. She was affectionate and funny and wasn't afraid to get her hair wet. She reacted well in an emergency. Kids were always scraping knees and falling out of trees.

She *deserved* to have the family she longed for. He couldn't hold her back from that.

It was a cold morning and she huddled in her windbreaker while Raj piloted them into the marina. It killed Everett to see her struggle to find a smile for the first mate as she thanked him and asked him to pass along her appreciation to the yacht's crew.

They were met by a bodyguard, Belle, whom Everett had already met online. She introduced herself to Bianca as part of Bianca's permanent detail. She was tall and had a wide jaw and a confident manner, but she shot a hard look off to her left as she was shaking Bianca's hand.

There was a small noise that could have been anything—a rub of a craft shoved hard against its mooring or something shifting and falling on the deck of a boat.

Everett's sixth sense was unbothered, which was the strangest thing. A few hours ago, he'd been prepared to keep Bianca on the yacht another day or two, his radar had been crackling so hard.

He had second-and third-guessed that impulse, wondering if he was merely finding an excuse to spend a little more time with her, but an hour ago, his tension had dissipated, leaving him with only the sick knot of having to say goodbye to a woman he was beginning to suspect he loved. Deeply.

"We used a decoy vehicle from the mansion to draw any followers, as you requested," Belle said to Everett in an undertone. "My partner is stationed at the top of the ramp and will let me know if he sees anything of concern." She touched her ear and smiled reassuringly at Bianca. "I swept the area before you arrived. It's a quiet day here."

Bianca looked at Everett, not the least facetious when she asked, "Do you think it's okay?"

He looked up the narrow leg of dock to where it joined the main stretch. Parts of it were cast in shadow by the luxury yachts in the slips on either side, but music drifted from some far-off craft and someone closer by was whistling tunelessly. There was a muted clink of equipment being moved around and the call of a gull.

"I do." He took her elbow and carried his own bag while Belle took Bianca's.

Walking up that swaying path felt a lot like slowly impaling himself on a spear. Was he being stubborn? Spineless? Or noble?

He wanted her to be safe and happy, and if he thought he could give her that, he would—

Belle touched her ear, dropped Bianca's bag and withdrew a gun.

Everett snatched Bianca into his chest and said with quiet urgency, "I love you."

She stumbled on the bag he dropped, but he held her upright, angling his body to shelter her from whatever bullets were about to rain down while he extended his other arm, pointing his own weapon at the men who appeared on the bows above them, all armed.

Six. Too many. Everett swore.

"You have a *gun*?" Bianca whispered into his chest, appalled.

"My partner has a clear shot," Belle warned them, but they all knew the men had the upper hand.

"No one will be shot today," one of the men said. "Let's put our weapons away, before someone calls the authorities and things become complicated."

"Did Ackerley hire you?" Everett demanded. He was like a granite statue, unmoving while his slamming heart bashed against Bianca's.

"No. We met him after he followed your car here from your home. We've removed him to another location. Your wife is perfectly safe, but my employer would like to meet her."

"Who is your employer?" Everett already knew and, judging by Bianca's muted gasp, so did she.

"Sandro Rodriguez."

She was shaking against him, but lifted her

face to say, "I don't want anyone to be hurt. Can you please all put those away?"

The one who had been speaking tucked his gun into the back of his waistband and showed his empty hands. "*Hermana.* Come. Bring your husband. This will only take a minute."

"You're not going anywhere," Everett growled, holding her so tight he might leave bruises, but apologizing for that could wait until he got her to safety.

"I'll go alone if you don't want to come," she said, voice solemn. "But I have to meet him, Everett. I have to."

"You don't even know if it's really him," he said through his teeth.

Another man appeared next to the one who had put his gun away.

Both Everett and Belle pointed their weapons at the new arrival. He was unfazed.

"Alejandra. Come. We only have a few minutes. I want to say hello." He had the firm tone of a parent who brooked no disobedience.

"Everett, please." She reached to touch his arm, silently urging him to lower his gun.

What could he do? Shoot her father? Refuse her this one chance and break her heart in an even more unforgivable way?

This was why he had never wanted to fall in love. It *was* terrifying. It meant allowing someone who meant everything to him to do something reckless and foolish, just because it made them happy.

He lowered his gun and let her come even with him so she could look up at her father.

Sandro's dark brown hair was gray at his temples and he had the slight paunch of middle age pressing against the button of his tailored jacket. His eyes were a world-weary version of hers, shaped like her own and—Bianca caught her breath and her eyes started to well as a slow smile of pride dawned on her father's lips.

"Come." Sandro beckoned. "You have time before your flight for one cup of coffee."

Thirty minutes later, Bianca collapsed shakily into the SUV.

Everett slid in behind her, shoving her across the cushions as he growled, "Get us the hell out of here."

Bianca didn't really register his anger. Her mind was still echoing with gruff, accented phrases. *You are so like her, with her staunch principles. I left her no choice, but I wish she had told me about you. I wouldn't have let you fall in with such a man as you did.*

It was such a fatherly thing to say.

The SUV took a sharp turn that had her tipping toward Everett, snapping her back to reality.

"I'm sorry. I know that put you in danger, but I really wanted to meet him and—"

Everett brushed her hand from the seat belt she was trying to buckle and gathered her into his lap. His arms were so hard around her, he was back to crushing her breath from her lungs.

"It wasn't me I was worried about." He was shaking.

"Everett, I'm *sorry.*"

"Stop apologizing. I know why you did it. Just… Be quiet while I process that we're still alive." His hands were moving on her as if searching for broken bones, but she was absolutely unharmed and feeling startlingly whole.

"What happened to your intuition? Why didn't you know that was going to happen?"

"Because you weren't in danger?" he snarled, then pressed his mouth to her hair. "That was the worst moment of my life, realizing I'd missed catching that we were surrounded."

She snuggled into his warmth, still in shock at finally meeting her father and one of her half brothers.

Lola had brought her existence to Sandro's attention. He'd read up on Bianca and had had people watching Everett's mansion for their return. When Troy turned up and followed the car to the marina, they had quickly disarmed him and "had a chat."

He won't approach you again. His partner is also aware that you are not without protec-

tion. Of course, you also have your husband to look after you.

Everett had said in a grave, warning tone, *She does.*

Had he also told her he loved her or had that been a terror-induced hallucination?

"I always feared he would reject me or resent me," she murmured. Instead, her father had been regretful of the years they'd missed while accepting that they had been necessary. They had ended with an agreement that it was best if their relationship remained distant.

My other children want to meet you, but that should wait for another time. You will tell me if you ever need anything, though.

I will, she had promised, because Sandro Rodriguez seemed like a man you didn't refuse.

"I know you're angry with me," she said to Everett, cuddling her shoulder beneath his arm. "But I'm grateful you let me meet him."

"I didn't have a choice, did I?" He kept his voice low to keep their conversation private from Belle and the guard in the driver's seat, the one she had yet to properly meet. "But don't ever do anything like that to me again."

"I'll live a very boring life of healthy eating and gentle exercise from now on," she assured him. "You won't have to worry about me."

"This isn't funny. I love you and I thought I was going to lose you. Let's both promise not to scare the hell out of each other if we can possibly help it."

"I wasn't sure if I heard you right the first time. In fact, I might need to hear it a few more times before it sinks in."

"I love you," he said in the most belligerently endearing way, she started to laugh.

And since she had so much tension built up, and he was scowling with so much annoyance, she laughed until her middle hurt.

Maybe it was cramps. She gave a final wistful sigh and relaxed her head onto his shoulder.

"I need to say something," she said. "What happened today was important to me. Even if I can't have much of a relationship with them, I needed to know I had that connection. With Mom's family gone, I needed to know I was a branch on someone's tree. Now I do. If you don't want to make a tree of our own, if you don't want children, I think I could live with that. I just want to be with you, Everett. I want that very, very much."

His chest shook as he took a big breath and let it out.

"You humble me." He cupped her face, tilting her gaze up to his. He caressed her cheek with his thumb and dipped his head to press his lips to her brow. "I want you to have whatever will make you happy, Bee, including the family you've always dreamed of. The stone-cold fact is, the more I think of you making babies with someone else, the more murderous I feel toward someone who doesn't even exist. If you're having babies, *I* will be their father. Take that to the bank."

Her heart was swelling in her chest, but it was catching on small, sharp hooks of concern. "I love that you're saying that, but I don't want you to have children unless you really want them. Don't say something like that to please me. Definitely don't make babies to please me. That's not fair to our imaginary children."

"I'm confident I would love our children a distressing amount. I'm fond of those little monsters of Giovanni's. I'm given to understand affection rises exponentially when it comes to one's own."

"Okay, well, we don't have to make that decision right now." She nuzzled her mouth into the warmth beside his Adam's apple. "Maybe we should get married first?" she suggested.

"There's an idea." He swore and patted for his phone, taking it out and grimacing as he flicked through his screens. "I already approved the press release that said we were taking a break. I'll see if I can catch it before it goes out."

"There's an idea," she mocked.

"I think that does it." He dropped his phone. "What were we talking about? Oh, yes. I was proposing. Will you marry me?"

"I asked you first."

"Then, yes. And soon. Very soon." He pressed their smiles together in a sweet kiss, one they kept reasonably PG on account of their audience.

After a moment, she said, "Maybe I should move into my own seat, now?"

"No, I'm not finished holding you. I don't think I ever will be."

That was convenient because she wasn't done being held.

EPILOGUE

One year later...

"I'M HOME!" BIANCA called as she walked into their New York penthouse.

Miami was their permanent home, but they traveled a lot, now that Everett had a consulting job with Roman Killian. He also had majority shares in an engineering firm working on electric car technologies. There was enough risk and challenge to keep him interested without being a threat to his wife's peace of mind.

Bianca was also in a very good place. The hearings over Morris and Ackerley were behind her. She had discreetly and tearfully met her half siblings a few months ago, and she had recently launched a marketing and branding business for romance authors. She had thought she might pick up one or two accounts, but she was already thinking of hiring an assistant to help her meet the demand.

"How was your day?" Everett asked, coming

into the kitchen where she was putting away the decaf coffee and vitamins she'd picked up on her way home. He looped his arm around her, kissing her temple.

"Good. Um—" She suddenly hit a wall of nervousness. She had told him she was meeting Freja for lunch today, which had been true, but she had also been to the doctor. Fortunately, she was able to delay spilling her news by pointing to the envelope on the counter. "You had a parcel downstairs."

"Oh, good. It got here in time. It's for you. I thought we might have a night in." He dragged the envelope across so it was in front of her, then leaned on the counter to watch her open it.

"A night in." She knew what that was code for and smirked as she pulled the tab on the envelope, amused excitement tingling through her.

Sometimes they still role-played and sometimes he liked to shop online for fresh story lines. Lately, he'd been going through a historical phase with a lot of pirates and dukes. It was a double win for her—great sex and something new to read in the bathtub when she had some downtime.

"Is it a werewolf? Because—" She grew speechless as she looked at the title.

"I thought I'd be the tech magnate if you want

to—" he tapped the cover "—drop your secret baby bombshell?"

She dropped the book. "I wasn't keeping it a secret! I just wasn't sure yet. How did *you* know?"

"Your body is like a clock, Bee. We stopped using protection three weeks ago and you're four days late. What else would it be?"

"I don't know, but I didn't expect it to happen on our first try!" She hugged herself, still in shock.

He took her by the arms, dipping his head to catch at her gaze. "Are you okay?"

"Yes. Ecstatic. But I wasn't sure how you—"

"I'm sure," he said, smiling with amused tenderness while a light of wonder grew in his eyes. "I feel like I swallowed the sun and I'm floating. Are you really pregnant?"

"Yes."

"God, I love you." He wrapped her in his arms and kissed her with such emotion, her eyes stung with tears behind her closed lids.

His own lashes were wet, and he self-consciously drew back and picked up the book to divert her from noticing how emotional he was.

"I think we just skipped the good part and ended up at happily-ever-after."

"That is the *good* part, silly. But I know how thorough you like to be." She pressed into him, running her hands from his shoulder blades to his backside, giving his buttocks a suggestive squeeze. "Let's go make sure we didn't miss anything."

They got it absolutely right.

* * * * *

Blown away by the magic of
Cinderella for the Miami Playboy?
Get caught in the drama of these other
Dani Collins stories!

Ways to Ruin a Royal Reputation
Her Impossible Baby Bombshell
Married for One Reason Only
Manhattan's Most Scandalous Reunion
One Snowbound New Year's Night

Available now!